T0246453

IF YOU KNEW MY NAME

A NOVEL IN VERSE BY
LISA ROBERTS CARTER

central
avenue

2024

Published by Central Avenue Publishing, an imprint of Central Avenue Marketing Ltd.
www.centralavenuepublishing.com

IF YOU KNEW MY NAME

978-1-77168-360-9 (pbk)
978-1-77168-361-6 (ebk)

Published in Canada
Printed in United States of America

1. YOUNG ADULT FICTION   / Novels in Verse
2. YOUNG ADULT FICTION   / Social Themes/Prejudice & Racism

1 3 5 7 9 10 8 6 4 2

Keep up with Central Avenue

ACT 1

On the Grind

MY MAMA is into all this BLACK LIVES MATTERS stuff.
She marches. She protests.
She wears BLM T-shirts like she's a walking billboard for the cause,
but she ain't doing it to get no applause
like some people who only want to be seen on TV.
My mama ain't got nothin' to prove.
She just got tired of seeing fatal police shootings of Black men
on the evening news.
So, she took to the streets
marching and sayin' their names.
Me? I just chill with my homies writing lyrics and creating beats.
We always on the grind. Got the mamba mentality.
They say good things come to those who wait — that's just a fallacy.
You got to stay on the grind if you wanna make it in the business.
Nobody gonna give you nothing. You gotta go get it.
That's what we out here tryna do,
                    EARN RESPECT,
make a name for ourselves.

See one day errbody gonna know our names.
Like when you hear the name Tupac Shakur or the Notorious B.I.G.
Maybe they not the best examples to use,
'cause them dudes was gunned down, but you know what I mean.
Rap music blew up when they arrived on the scene.
Dem boys had skills. Errbody has heard of 'em,
and just like them, errbody gonna know my name,
not the one my mama put on my birth certificate.
Mason's no rapper name, but it is a family tradition.

I'm a fourth-generation Mason.
I don't need no audition.
People in this city know I got game,
but what I need now is a stage name.
I'm a specialist. I ain't no general practitioner.
A rapper's name is his signature.
Whoever heard of the rapper LeSane?

NOBODY!

But that was Tupac's name before it was changed.
B.I.G. dropped the name Christopher.
Maybe his mama still called him Christopher.
I don't know, but on stage, he was the Notorious B.I.G.
And what about Calvin Cordozar Broadus Jr?
Calvin who?
That's what I said when I heard it too.
I said it got to be a family name for a dude to have a name like that,
but that's Snoop Dogg, yo.

Ain't nothing cool about LeSane, Christopher, or Calvin.
That's why when I make it big,
I'm gonna be known for an unforgettable handle
and an even better delivery,
a stage name that will go down in history.
I ain't thought of one yet,
but you best believe that I'm working on my signature.
The other members of my crew, Jay D
and Sultan (yep, that's his real name)
ain't gotta come up with no cool rapper names.
They got the kind of names that stick with you.

Jay D be slammin' with dem beats.

Even if you don't like to dance, he gon bring you to ya feet.

Sultan makes beats too.

He ain't as good as Jay D, but he working on his groove.

Sultan's name means King, so he wears a lot of bling.

He be fakin' it till he make it. He got a fake grill too.

Dude got so much bling in his mouth, he can barely keep it closed.

People laugh at him, but he smiles and says,

one day, it's gon be real gold.

My mama cool with me hanging with them

'cause they ain't no troublemakers or no dudes in the streets.

She laid down the law the first time they came over to cook beats.

Don't cuss in my presence.

Clean up after yourselves,

and don't go in my room for any reason.

You can't just come here doing your own thing.

Don't take anything you didn't bring.

   Jay D and Sultan ain't got no problems with MAMA'S RULES.

They ain't got sticky fingers,

and their mamas don't play about them being disrespectful.

Que — short for Quentin — wanted to join us,

I had to tell him no.

He good at creating beats and all,

but he would have broken Rule #1 the first day.

That joker got some sticky fingers.

If it ain't nailed down, he gon take it.

He creates beats for Nimrod, but he's a wannabe rapper,

spends most of his time freestyling in the park, nickel-and-diming people.

I seen people drop a few dollars in his fitted, but that just ain't my style.

I'm more into displaying my skills at battle raps.
My mama thinks that's a waste of time.
I showed her a couple of rappers' net worth.
She said you can't believe everything you read online
and that for every rapper that makes it,
there are thousands that try and fail,
and then she names famous rappers that are dead or in jail.

I ain't gonna be ANOTHER STATISTIC!

I'm gon make it. My boys gon be right there with me when I do,
spinning beats, packed-out shows with sold-out seats.
My mama worries about me too much.
She thinks that I'm another young Black man with pipe dreams,
like the kids who ain't never picked up a basketball
but say they gonna be the next Lebron James,
or the kids that sound like croaking frogs
that say they gonna be the next Beyoncé.
I ain't like them. I know I got skills,
but it takes more than skills to make it.
It takes hard work and dedication.
When you have a dream, you gotta want it more than anything.
That's me. I dream about rappin' all the time.
I go to bed with lyrics in my head and beats on my mind.
I design verses and beats in my sleep.
Creating is what I live, it's what I breathe, it's what I eat.

I gotta keep MY DREAM ALIVE.

I got to fight to keep from becoming another hashtag.
That's what my mama worries about the most,
that I'll become another targeted Black man,
like the dude who died only a few miles away from here.
He wasn't a gangbanger. He didn't have a criminal record.

He volunteered at a homeless shelter.
He didn't exactly fit the profile of the guy
the officer that fired the fatal shot described
as aggressive and confrontational.
Maybe that's what set the city on edge.

Hashtag

The morning after it happened,
people were blowing up my timeline with hashtags and comments,
calling for justice because another young Black man had been gunned down
by an officer of the law.
The Black man's one fatal flaw, the darkness of his skin.

    The truth is BLACKNESS IS THE BLACK MAN'S CRIME.
When he is killed by the men in blue, justice is blind.
He doesn't have to live the thug life to be profiled.
The latest hashtag was described as a family man with a wife and a child.
He was working his second job,
as a pizza delivery driver searching for an address that he never found
when an officer pulled him over for driving too slow
and accused him of casing the neighborhood.
A brother on the grind tryna make a living,
but because he Black, he gotta be up to no good.
Again, claims of justifiable deadly force are made,

                body cams lie,
    AND A BROTHER CAN'T SPEAK FROM THE GRAVE.

Accusations of resisting arrest are a common theme
when a Black person's taken in a body bag from the scene.
Personally, I had never heard of the guy whose picture frame
was behind today's "justice for" hashtag,
only that people were hashtagging his name
and saying they wanted justice because he had been slain.
I hashtagged his name too as if we were connected by bloodline,
knowing that if he doesn't get justice, one day his fate could be mine,
not that I want to become a hashtag,

but there's nowhere to escape when a simple traffic stop can escalate
into an explosion of gunfire,
or a chokehold can result in death
as you plead for your life
with your very LAST BREATH.
It doesn't matter whether you live on the East Coast or the West Coast,
in the North or in the South.
If you are Black in America, you already got a target on your back.
If you are Black in America, you live with the reality
that you are just one traffic stop,
one encounter while walking down the street,
one wakeup call in the middle of the night,
one bullet, one chokehold,
one knee to the neck from being a hashtag
or having strangers chanting your name.

#justicefor

#jacobblakelifematters

I wasn't there in Kenosha, Wisconsin,
when a police officer shot and wounded
Jacob Blake,
leaving him in a wheelchair.
I wasn't there when Kyle Rittenhouse fatally shot
demonstrators protesting police brutality,
and I wasn't at the Kenosha courthouse when Blacks
got another dose of reality
as Rittenhouse was acquitted of homicide.
The inequities in this case
was just another slap in the face.

#JusticeforFreddieGray

I wasn't in Baltimore, Maryland,
when Freddie Gray's spinal cord
was almost completely severed after he was handcuffed,
shackled, and thrown unbuckled in the back of a police van.
I wasn't there when he was denied immediate medical treatment
or when he told officers he couldn't breathe,
and I don't know if there are enough words
to put his mother's mind at ease
when she thinks about what happened to her son,
but I know what was done
to him wasn't right.

#justiceforgeorgefloyd

I wasn't in Minneapolis when George Floyd
allegedly bought cigarettes with a counterfeit twenty-dollar bill
or when Derek Chauvin made the decision to sit there and kneel
on George Floyd's neck for nine minutes and twenty-nine seconds,
but I watched the video that made so many cringe
and caused others to come unhinged,
that sparked protest and led to civil unrest.

#StopKillingUs

I wasn't in Atlanta when Rayshard Brooks
was fatally shot
by a police officer in the parking lot
of a Wendy's restaurant,
but that image of him being slain continues to haunt
me.
It's like cops get a free pass to kill Black people legally.

#BlackLivesMatter

I wasn't in Louisville, Kentucky,
when plainclothes officers
executing a drug search warrant
entered Breonna Taylor's apartment
after she had gone to bed and shot her eight times,
although there was no evidence
she had committed any drug crimes.

#JusticeforElijah

I wasn't in Aurora, Colorado,
when officers stopped Elijah McClain
because someone complained that he looked "suspicious and awkward."
I wasn't there when officers put him in a carotid hold,
or when he tried to explain that he was different.
You can't just kill somebody because they don't fit the mold
of how society thinks they should act or behave.
I wasn't there when he said he couldn't breathe
or when he was injected with ketamine,
or when officers took selfies reenacting a chokehold at his memorial site,
I wasn't there when the officers realized that Elijah had a mother
who loved him from the cradle to the grave
and was willing to fight
with all her might
for justice for her son.

#DrivingWhileBlack

I wasn't in Falcon Heights, Minnesota,
when Philando Castile
was shot and killed during a traffic stop.
I wasn't there when his four-year-old daughter cried
as she watched her dad's life slip away
right before her eyes.

#IfIDieInPoliceCustody

I wasn't at the Waller County, Texas, jail
when Sandra Bland
was found hanged in her cell
following what should have been
a routine traffic stop.
A death so strange, was suicide or foul play to blame?
A life forfeited all because of failing
to signal when changing lanes.

#handsupdontshoot

I wasn't in Ferguson, Missouri,
when Michael Brown
and his friend were walking in the middle of the street
and Officer Darren Wilson ordered them
to walk on the sidewalk.
Words exchanged. Situation quickly escalates
all because of a little trash talk.
Brown shot six times, including two bullets to the head
after witnesses said he put his hands up and shouted,
"Don't shoot."
The officer that mortally wounded Brown
said he never heard Brown say don't shoot,
but he wasn't deaf, and Brown wasn't mute.
I wasn't among the crowd that gathered
and watched as Michael Brown's bloodied body
lay in the street for four hours in the sweltering summer heat,
but I later marched among protesters with my hands raised, shouting,
"Hands up. Don't shoot!"

#ICantBreathe

I wasn't in Staten Island, New York,
when a brother minding his own biz,
not disturbing the peace,
tryna make a hustle was confronted by police
and placed in a chokehold.
Maybe Eric Garner was resisting arrest,
but I just don't believe the officer's story that not once,
out of eleven times, did he hear Garner say,
"I can't breathe."

#justicefortamir

I wasn't in Cleveland, Ohio,
when an officer in field training
shot twelve-year-old Tamir Rice at a park as he threw snowballs
and played with a toy pellet gun.
Maybe the officer really did think the gun was real,
but why not shoot to wound, not to kill?

#SayTheirNames

I wasn't there when any of these people drew their last breath,
but I was at the protest in Morgan Park when a Black man,
fortyish in age wearing a Black Lives Matter T-shirt
and jeans shouted into the megaphone in his hand,
"Say their names!"
Then he proceeded to rattle off a list of names,
some I was more familiar with than others,
like George Floyd and Breonna Taylor.
The scene was like watching a Black Lives Matter movie trailer.
The mixed multitude — which consisted of mostly Blacks,
some Whites and other ethnicities — roared in response,
resounding each name
like voices echoing through mountain terrain
until each victim had been recognized,
not for the hashtag they had become
but for the person their family and friends knew
before they began trending on Google, Bing, and Yahoo.
To be honest, I only went to the protest march
because Mama talked me into going.
I never meant to participate.
I was cool with being a spectator,
but something happened when I chanted their names
in unison with other demonstrators.
I realized I was a part of something greater
as I looked around and saw people of various shades
who had traveled near and far to tell the world
that these people who died at the hands of police mattered,
that their families were broken and shattered
by the loss of their loved ones,

that communities were divided because of misguided
perceptions that people of darker skin are inferior,
that their rights and lives are somehow of lesser value
than any other race, lies too many embrace.
Saying their names reminded me that they weren't just another hashtag
to add to a collection of hashtags calling for an end to police brutality.
They were mothers and fathers, sons and daughters.
They were friends and neighbors, coworkers and laborers.
They were loved and missed,
and they didn't deserve to be discarded and their killers rewarded
with a slap on the wrist.
Their voices had been silenced by violence.
Now we — the protesters — were their voices.

The Power of My Voice

When I left the BLM march, for the first time in a long time,
I thought about more than creating lyrics and beats.
I thought about the bruh that was killed by police on Lebanon Street.
I thought about his family, the distraught look on his mother's face,
the way his little sister wept on her daddy's shoulder
and said she wanted her brother back, and I wondered
how anyone would explain to her that he was killed because he was Black.
The more I thought about these things, the madder I became.
I thought about the use of excessive force
               and THE POWER OF MY VOICE,
and I wrote my name. Mason Zy'Aire Tyndall.
Then I wrote #MasonZy'AireTyndall.
Then I wrote #JusticeforMasonZy'aireTyndall.
I wrote every hashtag I had ever seen when I heard that
a Black person had been killed by a police officer
and I attached my name.
I thought to myself, how many times had I placed hashtags
in front of someone's name
without really thinking about
who was this person, or what they meant to their family and friends?
Did I hashtag because it was trending?
               WHAT MESSAGE WAS I SENDING?

That a person once so full of life
could be diminished to nothing more than social media strife.
Just when the guilt is gnawing at my insides
and my stomach is lurching like I've got jet lag,
Jay D sends me a copy of his class schedule,

reminding me that I need to choose an elective and fast.

There aren't many left to choose from.

Childcare is a definite pass.

Walk around campus burping a fake doll making sure that it poops.

Hopefully, Graphic and Web Design still has empty seats.

I ain't about to take accounting fundamentals

and spend my senior year learning Excel sheets.

If worse comes to worst, I'll opt for pottery class first.

Senior Year

It is my senior year.
The year I've waited for since I was a scrub back in middle school
when bag lunch and Velcro sneakers weren't cool,
and your mama put I-luv-u notes in your book bag,
and riding the bus to school was such a drag, just sad,
but you did what you had to do to get through
because you knew
that senior year was coming.
It is my senior year.
        The year that puts me at the top of THE FOOD CHAIN.
The year that I get to skip to the front of the line in the school caf
while poor, hungry underclassmen complain
that it ain't fair,
but they have no choice but to suck it up, stand back, and stare
as I get my tray and sit at one of the for-seniors-only tables
where larger-than-life tales are told
and the truth turns into fiction and fiction into fables.
It's the place where legends are made, and boys become men,
and masculinity is measured by the number of hairs on your chin,
and how often you've done it, with who, and when.
No one does a fact check
        because it's all about RESPECT FOR THE REP.
Yep! I'm not gonna lie.
Being a high school senior has its perks
like not getting your head dunked in toilets by jerks.
Not that it ever happened to me,
but I've seen it happen to others.
I'm just not down with dissing a bruh,

but you got upperclassmen punking underclassmen to build their stats.

Well, it's my senior year, and I got plans to
KICK BACK AND RELAX.

There's homecoming, senior prom, senior skip day, senior dance,
and the unforgettable senior class prank.
No one sweats getting caught
because in the hierarchy of high school, seniors pull rank.

Back-to-School Registration

It's back-to-school registration.
I have one objective in mind —
register for bird classes, so my senior year is a breeze.
Next year, it's official. I'll be an adult with adult responsibilities,
living on my own dime,
but in the meantime,
I got to get through my senior year.
I arrive at school around noon.
The front desk clerk peers over her glasses.
Her forehead creases like a prune.
"Your name," she says in a not-so-friendly nasal voice.
I want to walk back out the door,
but it's not like I have a choice;
if I want to graduate with my senior class I'll have to put up with the noise.
She hands me a registration card and tells me to take it
to my counselor, Ms. Franklin, who gives my card a quick glance over,
then keys in my information with her right pointer finger,
which can only mean one thing.
She can't type or at least she doesn't know the QWERTY keyboard,
but I can't afford
to make her angry, so I pass
at the opportunity to tell her that she could benefit
from a keyboarding class.
"You have all your math, language arts, science,
social studies courses," she says, "that just leaves your elective.
You are short a credit. Might I suggest
the Black poetry class.
No final exam required, not that you would fail a test."

I failed chem so she's throwing shade.

AN INSULT FOR AN INSULT, *a fair trade,*

but I won't go there just yet.

Sometimes my mouth gets me in situations I usually regret.

"Just a poem you create on your own," she continues.

"No plagiarism. That also means no help from friends or family at home.

This project must be completed alone.

We do not put restrictions on who, what, or where

your inspiration comes from

as long as they are your words."

Her forehead puckers as if something I'm doing is working her nerves,

then she says, "Young man, I'm gonna need you to spit out that gum."

Bingo. That's all she's mad about? It's cool, I'll toss it so we can move on.

She points to a wastebasket full of crumpled paper and pencil shavings.

She's a dinosaur, but who cares as long as I can get an easy A.

"Sure," I say,

annoyed that she's staring at me like I'm some dumb jock.

She glances at the clock

as she waits for my response.

"I'm not going to have to read about a bunch of old dead guys, am I?"

I spread my palms in a help-me-understand gesture.

"This is the first class of its kind at this school," she explains.

"I must warn you in advance

that administration has given your teacher a license

to incorporate materials that she believes will enhance

student learning."

By this time, my ears are burning.

"Poetry is not really my thing. What if I don't pass?

I won't have time to repeat the class."

"Are you the young man I heard rapping in the caf?

What do you think rap is if nothing but poetry?" she asks.

I LAUGH

to myself 'cause I know rap ain't hardly poetry,

but she insists it is poetry of sorts.

She's reaching, that's like saying playing chess is a sport,

but I humor her because she stands between me

and that black cap and gown with the gold tassel

so, I fall back, I don't give her no hassle.

"Rap is poetry about the ups and downs," she says.

"The highs and lows,

the woes

of life. Often written by poets

who don't even recognize that they are poets."

"Poetry and rap aren't the same,"

I tell her.

She sighs. "What a shame

you don't know that some of the most famous rappers

were poets."

"Yeah. Name one," I challenge.

"Tupac Shakur. What do you know about him?" she asks.

"He was a rapper who got shot in the street.

The dude had real skills."

"Hmph," she shakes her head. "Take a seat."

She points to a chair that had worn out its wear.

"What I remember about Tupac," she says, "is that he wrote

'THE ROSE THAT GREW FROM CONCRETE.'

Now you may think a poetry class could have no bearing on your

future as an aspiring rap artist,

but you are wrong.

Add a few beats to rap music and you've got poetry in song,

but if you want to waste your time taking a class

just so you can pass,

I can sign you up for any of a number of courses:

culinary arts, auto mechanics, or fashion and design.

Maybe they'll help you fulfill your dream."

"Don't you think you're being extreme?"

I stand to my feet.

"I don't need a poetry class. I can spit lyrics while counting sheep

in my sleep."

"Why do people buy throwbacks?" she asks.

That's a no-brainer. "'Cause they cheap."

"Do you want to live the life of a throwback rap artist?" she continues.

"A throwback rap artist. Ain't no such thing."

"You rapped at a few clubs.

Now it's gone to your head.

Mason, if you're not willing to hone your craft,

your career is DOA before you get out of bed."

"So, you heard me rap a little, but you should see me drop the mic,

and then tell me how much I need a poetry class."

"I'M DONE TALKING." She claps her hands together.

"But you should know the electives I mentioned are filling up fast,

so, pick your poison. What will it be?"

She taps her claw-like fingernails on the desk.

"I have another student waiting to see me."

"Okay," I mumble. "I'll take the stupid poetry class.

Just sign me up before I change my mind."

Her lips curl upward.

"Ms. Jordan is not the type of teacher to give makeup work,

so, make sure you turn your assignments in on time."

"Ms. Jordan? I ain't never heard of her."

"That's because she is new here, but she is not new to teaching."
I can tell Ms. Franklin IS REACHING,
but I nod compliantly.

Now that registration is complete,
I can focus on my beats.
I'm still not crazy about the idea of taking a poetry class,
but there's no way
I'm going to walk around campus all day
holding a doll for the guys to rag on me and for the girls to brag on me.
I'm not down with the baby daddy jokes.
A few of the guys at Dickerson High already have kids.
I'm not about to play them,
but I'm not ready for that kind of responsibility.
I like spending my money on me.
I like buying the latest kicks, and Apple electronics.
I don't have time for potty training and teaching phonics.
Besides, I have to get ready for Nae's party.
Jontrae has challenged me to a battle rap.
Jontrae is an unsigned hype.
You probably have met his type.
He has been rapping since he was big enough to hold a toy microphone.
He ain't on the professional level just yet, but he can hold his own.
I GOT TO BRING MY A-GAME when I battle Jontrae.
He got a tight rep, but I ain't afraid.
He don't compete unless he get paid.
Me? I ain't like that. You just tell me where and when.
I been rapping since I was ten.
My love for rap started after
I heard these dudes going at it with each other right

on the street corner in front of Mr. Zullo's electronic store,
and this dude with them was beatboxing.
It was the coolest thing I had ever witnessed.
Right then, I knew what I wanted to do with my life.
My first shot at battle rapping happened a year later.
Some guys were freestyling at the park.
I decided to give it a shot.
I earned credits my first time out,

    LEAVING NO DOUBT that I got what it takes
to be a rap artist,
but I'm hoping to do more than earn credit at Nae's party.
I heard sometimes promoters show up.
Maybe I'd get a deal like Hashtag did when he rapped
at Lil Petey's B-Bash and earn some serious cash.

Battle Rapping in My Dreams

Jay D sends me a text telling me to check out one of Nimrod's tweets.
I log in to my account, but MY EYELIDS ARE HEAVY,
and my body needs sleep.
My mind is still charged. I'm in a trippy state.
I got some competition to eliminate,
creating lyrics as I slumber.
Nimrod the hunter 'bout to be a runner.
I'm dropping the mic like there's no tomorrow.
My homeboy Jay D creating beats like he's in the Congo.
Crowd getting bigger.
Now Nimrod is ready to reconsider
the drop-the-mic challenge he made on Twitter,
but I'm not backing down. I'VE NEVER BEEN A QUITTER.
He's whining like a toddler. Maybe I need to call him a sitter.
He got a frog in his throat. His lips all chap.
I can tell he ain't never been to a battle rap.
Knees buckling. He is struggling for words,
sounding like a flock of tweeting birds.
I'm not boasting, but just when I'm roasting Nimrod
like a leg of lamb, and he's trying to figure out
how to get out of this jam,
my cell phone rings, interrupting my dream.
It's Kaesan.

Nae's Back-to-School Kickback

He has been blowing me up all morning.
My guess is he wants to talk about Nae's back-to-school kickback.
It's a BYOB-drop-the-mic kind of party,
and a chance to show off your new BAE,
if you have one, that is.
>   *At the moment, I'm flying solo, but*
>   *THAT'S ABOUT TO CHANGE.*
Allow me to explain.
My ex said she needed a commitment
like what we had wasn't enough.
She wanted a ring of all things to make it official or she was done.
It's been fun,
but I'm not ready to put a ring on it.
This is our senior year of high school, not our senior year of college.
>   *NOBODY is going to hold me hostage*
to a relationship,
so, I decide it is time for me to dip.
The summer was over before it got started,
and I'm still on the hunt to find a honey to chill with til I go to college.
Kaesan and I are about the only guys that aren't boo'd up.
As I am going through my phone contacts, Kaesan interrupts
me with an S.O.S. text saying he needs my advice.
So, I put my thoughts on ice
and call him to see why he keeps blowing up my line.
Kaesan wants to know my thoughts about Cassidy Leonard.
I tell him the truth.
She ain't no dime piece.
Cassidy is my neighbor; she's Ms. Kelly's niece.

Ms. Kelly always has good things to say about her,
but I think Kaesan can do much better.
When he says that he is thinking about asking her out,
I have to know, "Is your rep that bad that you want to date a sideliner?"
"She ain't ugly," says Kaesan.
"No," I say, "but she plain, too plain."
"She's natural," Kaesan defends Cassidy's kinky coils and natural eyelashes.
"She doesn't need makeup and weave."
                    "Man don't be so NAÏVE."
I don't want to diss him if he's feeling her, so I say,
"What do you know about her besides the fact
that she's the only girl in high school who doesn't wear lash extensions?"
"We worked together as summer camp counselors," he says.
"She may not have the prettiest face, but she has all the right dimensions.
Besides that, she is cool, not like mad cool, but she has dope conversation."
                    "Do you bruh." I say, "DO YOU."
"That's the thing, she's not really me," Kaesan replies,
"but I like her." That's when I realize
that Kaesan isn't just looking for someone to get boo'd up with.
His choice took me by surprise,
but I ain't mad at him.
"Are you going to ask her to go with you to Nae's party?" I ask.
"I'm thinking about it," he says, "but I don't want nobody clowning her.
She's not the type you take to a party," he says.
"She's more like the kind of girl you take to the library."
Kaesan ain't sure what to do, so I tell him straight up.
"If she gonna be your shawty, then you can't let nobody diss her.
You have to shut that down.
You're either in or out of the relationship.
There's no middle ground."

x

"Word," said Kaesan.

I arrive at Nae's party with nothing in hand.
Some of the guys are checking me out
because this is a BYOB — Bring Your Own Booze — type of affair.
Nae's parents won't purchase alcohol for underage drinkers,
so, if you want anything stronger than cola,
you have to bring your own beverage.
"Man, what's going on? I don't see nothing in your hands," says Castille,
"and your pockets are too small."
Castille knows I don't drink. That was my uncle's downfall.
A DUI cost him fifteen years of freedom and a teenage girl's life,
       A BIG-TICKET DECISION for a temporary high.
"Man, I'm just messing with you," Castille laughs.
"I know you don't drink, but I'm gonna get wasted."
He nods to Kenyatta. "She already knows to take my keys
and call me an Uber."
I pat him on the shoulder. "Smart maneuver."
Castille looks around. "Hey man, where's your shadow?
Don't tell me that you're here solo."
"Jasmine and I are done."
"What about you, Kaesan? You got a date?"
Kaesan looks over at Cassidy, who is standing by the punch bowl.
"Cassidy is your date?" Castille raises his brow.
"Yeah. She's my shawty," Kaesan says with a smile.
"Cool." Castille shrugs,
then starts talking about my freestyle
and how I must be crazy for accepting Jontrae's battle challenge.
Jontrae has a rep that gives his comp the chills,
but he's not the only one with skills.

Castille says he heard a producer is gon be at the battle rap.
What if this rumor is all part of a dramatic plot to scare me?
Could be. I don't know,
but what I do know is that I got to SHOOT MY BEST SHOT.
"Thanks for the heads-up," I say.
We give each other dap. Castille leaves me standing there in dismay
while he follows some ratchet chick in white booty shorts and fake
Michael K's.
She ain't Kenyatta. I ain't never seen her before,
but she looks like trouble with a capital T.
I have a theory
about what's going to happen when Kenyatta sees Castille
talking to her.
As my mama would say, "It ain't gon be pretty; that's for sure."
Kaesan ain't really listening. He's too busy checking out Cassidy.
If falling in love was a crime, Kaesan would be doing serious time.
Cassidy walks toward us with two cups of punch in her hand.
Kaesan says he gotta go,
leaving me solo.

Nae's Back-to-School Bash

I came thirty minutes early to scout out the honeys.
Competition is stiff. Guys spitting game left and right.
Borrowing their daddy's Benz or renting luxury cars
to impress girls instead of taking a Lyft.
I can't say that I blame them.
No one wants to go through their senior year solo.
It's so not cool. It's like getting played or stood up,
so I got to hook up with somebody tonight.
I look around the room to see who is fine and who is presentable,
ANYTHING LESS, I ain't feeling them.
Diamond is holding down the wall.
My guess is she can't dance.
She standing there all cute but guys passing by,
not even giving her a second glance.
She's almost a dime, like a nine out of ten fine.
Girl got the looks, but she into her books,
so guys put her in the presentable category.
Presentable girls are the ones you hook up with
after there ain't no more fine girls to choose from at the party.
They look alright, but like my Southern-born daddy says,
they ain't nothing to write home to Mama about.
Diamond glances at me and looks away
like she doesn't want to make it obvious that she's feeling me,
but I can tell that she is. I walk up to her and ask if she wants a drink.
She smiles and says she'd like some punch,
then adds that she doesn't drink. "Neither do I,"
"Really?" she replies. She doesn't believe me.
"Seriously, I've never touched the stuff," I say.

LYING BETWEEN MY TEETH

I hold back that I had bourbon before my uncle's accident
and that I used to sneak my dad's beers out of his cooler.
"Oh." She half-shrugs.
"I don't touch the stuff. My mom drinks enough for the both of us."
"Bummer," I reply. "I'll get that punch for you."
I tell the fat guy guarding the punch
that I don't want anything that's been spiked.
He nods and points to a green bowl.
I pour two cups and head back over to Diamond.
Gentry standing in front of her with one hand propped against the wall.
She looks uncomfortable, but she is much too nervous
to tell him to get up out of her face, so I do it for her.

He gives me the EVIL EYE before mumbling and walking away.
"Thanks," she says.
"Here's your punch."
"It's not spiked, is it?"
"Nah. I wouldn't do that to you."
"I heard you're participating in the battle rap tonight."
"Yeah. Have you heard me rap before?"
"Around campus."
"Is this your first battle rap?"
"No. I've done them before, but this is my first with Jontrae."
"He's good."
"I didn't know that battle raps were your thing."
"They aren't. Jontrae was at my brother's birthday party."
"That's what's up, but you could have invited me to battle rap."
"Kingston made out his own guest list."
"He must not have heard about me."
"You're A LEGEND, right?"

"That's my battle rap name."

"I thought you earned it as a player."

"Nah. It ain't even like that.

I ain't trying to make a name for myself as a player."

"Well, maybe you ought to tell that to some of the girls who are
fighting over you."

"I ain't dating nobody." I shake my head.

"I believe they call it sneaky linking."

"So now you got jokes. You're funny. I like that."

Two hours into the party and an hour of nonstop
conversation with Diamond,

SOMEONE SHOUTS BATTLE RAP,

followed by another and then another,

and before I realize what is happening, the emcee announces,

"Jontrae and Legend will be battling tonight."

Since Jontrae challenged me, I get to go first.

"See you after the battle," I say to Diamond.

"You're going to stick around to watch me drop the mic, aren't you?"

"Sure." She smiles as if she doesn't believe I stand a chance
of dropping the mic on Jontrae.

Now I'm lowkey starting to doubt, but it's too late to back out,

so I leap on the stage like I KNOW I GOT THIS.

The instrumentals start. I'm feeling the rhythm of the beats.

I look at Jontrae's head, and I decide to start with that.

The Battle Rap

Mason

Your dome is big, but your brain is so small.
I don't think I have time to explain; you're not grasping it all.
I'm what you call legendary.
A word too complex, you can't even carry.
I would let you check the definition in the dictionary.
But with your limited vocabulary,
Bro you gon need a Pictionary.

Jontrae

You're one to talk about somebody's head
When yours is literally shaped like an egg.
And it contains no knowledge, no wonder you didn't know
Bet I could crack your forehead it would spill out a yolk
As for "Legendary," what a delusional claim
I'd be surprised if ya mama and ya daddy even remember ya name
Listen, you came home from school and had ya mama in shock
She was trippin thinking a kid had got off on the wrong block
Even told the bus driver he'd let you off at the wrong stop
When you refused to leave, she had to call in the city cops
You still wouldn't budge, so they had to call in the whole SWAT.

Mason

Speaking of moms, I saw yours in Walmart.
It took me by surprise, she was shopping with two carts.
I said to myself, well I guess that's kind of smart,
Buying grocery once a month makes sense
When you got a lot of mouths to feed,

You do what you gotta do out of necessity, not greed.
My heart was filled with sorrow
For the struggling single mom
Until she hollered back at the cashier and said, "See you tomorrow!"

Jontrae

Yo, this dude really out here reaching for family drama
Well let me put you on blast about all your daddy's baby mamas
There's Rosemary with the twins and Jen with the one
Keisha and Moneisha, yeah they each got a son
Let's not forget Fran, she's his favorite one
The whole town know how that lady get down, she always fighting
And your silly old man went out there and had three kids by her
When ya daddy get paid he tell the bank teller to keep quiet
Cus he owe child support and he don't wanna get indicted
So my mama might struggle, yeah I'll give you that
But if it wasn't for ya mama, boy y'all wouldn't have jack.
It's really so sad that your daddy can't stay away from that sugar shack!

Mason

Bruh, that was so weak.
Why you had to come for my dad with your critique?
Let's keep it between us, no need for the family heat.
But since you movin' a lil slow, I'll give you this one for free.
5486 Bellmore Street, that's the address to Walmart
Go in and run straight to aisle three
Once you get there buy five cans of Axe and ten sticks of Degree
Cus ya pits so musty, boy I'm standing next to you and can barely breathe.
On that note, I'd say this battle is over
I'll take the win and you can go ahead accept defeat.

Jontrae

Nah, bruh. I'm just getting started.

How you gonna talk about hygiene when ya breath is so pungent

Every time you speak a bar my whole stomach start turning

And when's the last time that you wash them funky boxers?

Guess ya mom only had bread for one pair, you got limited options

While we on the subject of hygiene, what's up with dem nappy dreads?

If you think you won this battle then

You must've really let them lil Medusa snakes go straight to ya head

'Cause everybody knows I'm the best of the best

But be my guest since you tryna put a lil hair on ya chest.

Mason

Ay, I ain't the one with the messed-up grill.

That plaque in your mouth looks like a tub of Country Crock

Met a gallon of buttermilk.

Look, I'm just keeping it one hundred percent.

In case you don't know what a toothbrush is,

It's the thing with the handle and bristles on the end.

Yo' breath smells so bad, even a skunk won't stand downwind.

Jontrae

What'd you say? I was napping.

Ya rap game lame. It ain't nothing but cappin'

You claim to be a legend, but that's just a name.

Skills are what matter, and yours are not in my lane.

I could try to educate you, but it's a waste of my time.

So step aside while I decide who's next in line.

Cus you just flicking while the clock keeps ticking.

I'm a pro at what I do, what I have is what you're missing

See while you hanging with ya boys on the game all day
I'm chipping at my craft and putting work behind my name.

I see you're still confused. Okay, I'll clarify.
When it comes to rap skills, you're in short supply.
So take notes from the GOAT because this is how you rap a battle.
With skills sharp like a knife and bars that rattle.
I've seen some sad things, but there is nothing sadder
Than your rap skills.
Now clean up my stage while I continue to climb my ladder.

Jontrae drops the mic.
The crowd jeers and some boo me off the stage,
But I take my loss like a man. I can't allow Jontrae to see me sweat.

Castille slaps me on the back. "That was brutal."
"Tell me about it." I shake my head.
"Better luck next time," he says.
Frederick, Castille's neighbor, weighs in.
"Luck ain't gonna help you against Jontrae," he says.
Castille cuts his eye at Frederick
'cause me and Frederick don't roll that way.
There are some things that only your homie can say,
not unless they want to get popped in the mouth.
"I tried to tell you that you weren't ready for Jontrae,"
says Castille.
Castille talks too much, but he got my back.
I walk off while he's talking 'cause I see Kenyatta headed our way,
and she madder than a driver with road rage being cut off on the freeway.
Her temper's high and her patience is low;

she's got that look in her eye that it's time to let him know.
I leave them to have at it. I ain't got time for that.
I still got to get a hookup
before the first day of school.

 AIN'T NOTHING COOL about being solo your senior year.
Like it's okay to be a player freshman, sophomore, and junior years,
but when you are a senior, you have to shift gears.
It's your last year of high school.
Nobody remembers you if the only photo of you
is your senior year pic.
Seniors that are remembered dominate the yearbook with
sports, fashion, and cute couple pics.
As I'm pondering my limited dating options,
and how I need to make a move
 to be FOREVER REMEMBERED by my classmates,
I spot Diamond in her fire girl kicks.
Never figured her for a sneakerhead chick
but those sneakers just dropped.
And only real sneakerheads gets the latest cop.
So, I have no doubt that she's a true sneakerhead.
But whether she is into dread heads, I don't know.
 She hung around to WATCH ME FLOW.
So maybe I got a chance.
"You're still here," I say.
"I told you I would stay until the battle rap was over."
She flashes a smile that makes me weak in the knees.
No girl ever had this kind of effect on me.
I glance at the keys in my hand and then at the door.
"Do you need a ride home?" I ask.
"My brother is picking me up," she says.

"I can give you a ride home if you'd like."

Diamond raises her brow In A Suspicious Slant.

"Just a ride home," she says, "nothing else."

I pant, pretending to be thirsty, then laugh. "Nothing else," I say.

"If you try anything, my brother is going to beat you into a coma,"

Diamond replies with a smirky smile.

"Okay." I grimace, shoving my hands in my pockets.

"I'll keep my eyes on the road the entire ride

because being unconscious in the presence

of a cutie like you ain't exactly my style."

Old Skool vs New Skool Rap

Riding down the highway with my car in cruise control.
I'm tapping my steering wheel as my favorite artist is rapping.
Diamond looking out the window like she's on an airplane.
"Could you turn that down?" she asks.
My plans to impress her just went down the drain.
Diamond is different from any girl I have ever dated.
She is a head turner for sure, but if you ask me,
pretty is overrated.
I've met enough girls with cute faces and empty heads.
Diamond is smart. I like that about her.
But she isn't feeling my music, so I have to ask,
        "WHAT'S WRONG with my rap?"
"Are you in a hurry?" she asks. "This could take all night."
As she folds her arms across her chest, I do my best
to focus my gaze on her face.
After all, she's the type of girl that carries mace.
"You for real?" I playfully scoff.
"Yes. I'm for real," she scolds me with her eyes.
        "Everyone is entitled TO THEIR OPINION,"
        I shrug, "even if it's off."
She nods. "For starters, I don't like the way rap degrades women."
"Okay," I agree, although that's a given.
"Some rappers degrade women in their songs, but not all rappers.
What else?" I ask.
"The language is so raw with residual effects.
It contains too much violence, profanity, and sex.
Not to mention, it glamorizes destructive behavior."
"Wait a minute," I interrupt.

47

"Rap isn't about finding A HERO OR A SAVIOR.
It's about defining life for what it really is."

"I wouldn't want my little sister listening to it," she continues.

"Let me guess, you prefer old skool rhythm and blues," I tease.

"Boy, please." She slips me a smile.

"I prefer smooth jazz jams.

Jazz music is therapeutic. It's relaxing. It helps me focus on my studies."

Jazz is cool, but I wish Diamond felt differently
about modern rap, but she thinks it's cap.

Most of it isn't rated PG-13, but it's not all bad.

I want to prove to Diamond that she is wrong
about contemporary rap.

If only she'd give me a chance
to get to know her while she got to know my music.

I am good at thinking quick on my feet.

"Can I take you to dinner or a movie or both?" I ask.

"I promise that it'll be lit."

"I've decided not to date my senior year," Diamond explains.

"A smart girl sees a cute guy and forgets about her grades.

Just like that, he persuades her to spend more time
with him than in her books.

Not me. I REFUSE TO BE DISTRACTED
by sweet talk and good looks."

"That's why one of the prettiest girls in the school doesn't have a boyfriend.
You're so quick to put them in the wind."

"I know what guys say about me." Diamond snaps her head to one side.

"They call me basic. You've probably called me that too."

"Uh. Rating girls is something guys do.

I'm not saying it's right, but IT HAPPENS."

"Hey, it's no big deal. I've called you a few names too."

"Really?" I say, trying to maintain my cool.

"No," Diamond laughs. "I just wanted to see the look on your face."

PRICELESS.

I confess, I like her vibes, but she has sworn off guys

at least for her senior year.

So how do you get to know someone who won't let you near?

Diamond thanks me for the ride home.

I thank her for watching me get my butt kicked.

SHE LAUGHS softly.

Her dimples appear as if they have been waiting

for an invitation to make me wonder

why I had never noticed them before tonight.

I lean across her to unbuckle her seat belt. She flinches.

"IT'S ALRIGHT.

It gets stuck sometimes," I explain, freeing her from the seat belt's grip.

"Oh," she says, "I thought you were trying to give me a kiss."

"Nah! And risk being put in a coma, I don't think so."

Her lips curve upward into a broad smile,

deepening her dimples. I walk her to the door,

get back in my car and drive away.

I would start my first day of my senior year solo.

A Rep to Defend

Tonight, things didn't go as planned,
and now Jontrae flossing.
I didn't get the girl,
but it is not the end of the world.
So what if I lost the battle rap.
Jontrae hasn't seen the last of me and neither has Diamond.
Drop-the-mic battles happen all the time,
                    but Diamond is ONE OF A KIND,
and I can't get her dimpled cheeks off my mind.
Jontrae would be back. This was far from the end
of the story. I have a rep as a rapper to defend my glory
and a rep as a player to lose,
but first I have to get through a poetry class
that may not be ready for my views.

Creative Writing Class Rm 104

A young White woman with a warm smile, soft brown eyes,
and long loose curly brown hair draped over one shoulder
walks through the door.
She has olive skin like the Kardashians.
"I must be in the wrong class,"
I say, handing her my late hall pass.
She takes my registration sheet from my hand,
gives the form a quick glance,
and confirms that I am in the right class.
"But . . . " I protest, feeling a little stressed.
"Is there a problem?" She shakes her head slightly.

"A big one. YOU'RE WHITE."

A Caucasian teacher teaching a Black poetry class
just don't feel right.
"And you're being a jerk,
but I'll try not to hold it against you." She smiles.
Her looks clash with her attitude.
I check out her fit.
She down with the current styles.
She could probably give some of the girls
at this school a few fashion tips,
but she ain't here to teach fashion,
and since writing lyrics is my passion,
I need to know if she believes in

FREEDOM OF EXPRESSION.

I got to do me.
If I'm gonna write about being Black,
I can't have nobody riding my back,

telling me what I can and cannot say

'cause I live the Black experience every day.

Ain't nobody gon tell me what it feels like to be me.

"Ms. Franklin never said that you were White," I say.

"Isn't that like misrepresentation,

a White teacher teaching a Black history class?"

          "I never misrepresented myself," Ms. Jordan

          DEFENDS HER POSITION.

"I love teaching creative writing, but I did not approach

anyone about a Black poetry class.

However, when the school presented me with this opportunity,

    I didn't say, 'I can't teach a Black poetry class because I'm White.'

Teaching is what I do.

Now if you want to learn how to master techniques

that will help you improve your writing, then take a seat,

but if not, I suggest you drop the class."

"Are you always this raw?" I ask.

"Mr. Tyndall, in this class, you will learn

the true meaning of being raw."

"What's that supposed to mean?"

          "It means you will learn about

          FREEDOM OF EXPRESSION IN WRITING."

"I can handle that," I say.

"Well, that remains to be seen."

She looks at me as if she is creating a mental profile.

"With freedom comes responsibilities," she says.

"I don't want to be a journalist. I'm a rapper," I reply.

Ms. Jordan chuckles softly.

I want to ask what's so funny,

but I remind myself that I need this class to graduate,

so I keep my cool,

lay low and GO WITH THE FLOW.

Avoiding eye contact, I walk to my seat.

The chatter stops.

JAWS DROP.

Students looking like they're saying what is he doing in here.

Jaquesha can't seem to take her eyes off me, so I say,

"Anybody ever tell you that it's rude to stare?"

Ladarius looks back. "What's up, homie?" he says.

"It is what it is," I tell him.

He nods like he understands

that I'm not feeling this class.

I pass Tayvion.

He used to battle rap, but now he's into balling.

He doesn't notice me.

He's busy palming a basketball while trying to spit game

to Lynesha. Them lines so played out.

She is looking at him like, boy that's lame,

then she breaks out with a big grin.

Yep, he is reeling her in.

I know most of the students who signed up for the poetry class.

There's Jasmine — the blacker than Black girl with the whiter than
White girl's hair,

platinum blonde to be exact —

and her sidekick DeAndre. Don't even make me go there.

He trying to live the BEST OF BOTH WORLDS,

low key swapping lip liner with the girls

while trying to flex at the gym.

Are you into her or into him?

Mixed messages it seems.

I'm not down with dissing a bruh
even if we ain't kicking it like that.

    Someone once said LIVE AND LET LIVE.

Me, I just keep it positive
and keep it moving.
The White dude sitting at the back of the room
looking all confused
like he's wondering if he should drop the class too.

  I can tell he ain't ready to hear about WHITE PRIVILEGE

and the truth about how this country was really built.
I stare at him.
He lowers his gaze.
Nothing but guilt.
And then there's the other White boy.
He looks like he should be holding a MAGA sign.
Everything about him screams racist.
Hitler haircut, the callousness in his eyes.
Dylann Roof come to take us by surprise,

    BUT I GOT MY EYES ON YOU.

Ain't gonna be no repeat of Emanuel Nine.
Just as I am taking my seat, in walks a third White boy,
he joins the others at the back of the room,
his reason, strength in numbers, I presume.
And then there's the Hispanic dude
mean mugging me like he not in the mood

    to hear what I got to say about
    THE BLACK EXPERIENCE,

or any other Black students for that matter.
I can tell that he just wants to be left alone
'cause he got serious problems of his own

like wondering whether some of his undocumented family and friends
are going to be deported if they are reported.

I got no beef with illegals.

Traveling hundreds and thousands of miles on foot and by sea,
buying fake IDs might seem extreme,

but who doesn't want to live
THE AMERICAN DREAM?

Then there is Ladarius flexing gang tattoos,

but it doesn't take long to figure out

that he got a few loose screws.

He can go from zero to one hundred just like that

in less than ten seconds flat.

I steer clear of the dude. He's a wannabe gangbanger.

He ain't the real deal, but he got gang ties.

To make him mad wouldn't be wise.

I ain't got time to be WATCHING MY BACK,

never knowing when or where you're gonna be attacked.

There are three White girls in the class.

I'm already prepared to put the "Karens" on blast.

There's Kabria, trapped between two worlds,

half Black, half White.

Don't know where she fit in.

I'm guessing she figured this class is a good place to begin.

Fajah and Khalan, Black power all day long.

Jamir and Zaquaisha got this toxic connection.

One minute they off. The next they on.

Ms. Jordan closes her classroom door and instructs the class

to take our seats.

She isn't at all like what I imagined.

Besides being White, she's fine, like *Sports Illustrated* swimsuit model fine.

Most teachers at Dickerson been here since the dinosaur age.
They ain't even on the same page
as this generation.
They still remember the days of televisions on rolling carts,
chalkboards, and film projectors.
They're not cool with out-of-the-box teaching and technology education.
I can tell from the rook piercing and tiny rose gold nose stud
Ms. Jordan IS A REBEL.

The Power of Choice

"Good afternoon, I'm Ms. Jordan."
Tayvion's right brow shoots upward.
"Is that Miss, as in single?" he asks.
Lynesha rolls her eyes hard.
Tayvion knows Ms. Jordan is out of his league,
but he gon run the play even if he don't gain no yards.
"We have twenty students in this class," Ms. Jordan continues.
"I expect to hear from all of you.
                    NO ONE IS INVISIBLE in this class.
Participation is required.
Just because this is an elective does not guarantee you will pass
this course.
You will be given the grade you earn,
so with that said, I hope you came to learn."

A knock at the door interrupts Ms. Jordan's speech.
Principal Martin introduces a new student.
The girl wheels past him in search of a place
to park her chair. She finds a space
to the right of Ms. Jordan's desk near the second window.
She locks her wheels, lifts the footplates, and extends her spindly legs.
I can't help but notice the bulbous scar just above her right elbow.

In her lap is an oversized canvas tote bag with the stitching "Emma."
She reaches into the tote, pulls out a metal tube and clear tray.
After connecting the tube to the arm of her chair,
she clamps the tray onto it, creating a portable laptop desk.
"That's what's up," says Ladarius.

The girl looks at him as if she's trying to determine
if he is serious or joking.
"Just ignore him," I tell her, "he's a work in progress."
"I'm just saying it's pretty cool the way
you don't let your condition bother you."
"You think?" The girl shakes her head.
"You know it's got to bother her. She used to be a cheerleader.
Now she can't even walk, and her boyfriend dumped her,"
says Zaquaisha.
The girl's cheeks turn crimson red.
"The name is Emma. I can't walk, but my hearing is fine.
You don't need to be concerned about me.
You need to be concerned about your receding hairline."

"Oh snap," Ladarius shouts. "White girl throwing shade."
Zaquaisha mumbles something and looks away,
embarrassed because she just got her hair slayed
in a top braided ponytail with the gold dreadlock beads
and fake lace baby curls.

Zaquaisha got traction alopecia
from wearing tight weaves and braids,
but she's not the only Black girl around school
disguising thinning edges.
Some girls use edge gel, swoops and bangs,
but the goal is the same —
hide the bald spots.
I pretend not to notice 'cause the truth is
when you talk about a Black girl's hair, you gonna see fangs.

Principal Martin leaves.

Ms. Jordan closes her classroom door.

Lynesha springs to her feet.

"Ms. Jordan, I'm finna go off.

New girl just dissed Quay about her hair.

I don't care if she is in a wheelchair,

nobody gonna play my friend like that."

          "RESPECT. You do not have to like one another,"

says Ms. Jordan.

"But if you are to remain in this class

to the end of the semester, you will respect one another."

Ms. Jordan continues her overview.

"As you may have already guessed, learning Black poetry

means learning Black culture.

This is a creative writing class which also means you will create poetry."

Ms. Jordan holds up a book.

Lynesha takes her seat but not before giving

Emma the watch-it-White-girl look.

Emma blows a raspberry with some added eye language in return.

If looks could burn,

Lynesha would go up in flames.

"There are no assigned seats,"

says Ms. Jordan, "however, you will keep the seat you chose today

for the next week or for as long as it takes me to learn your names."

My gaze shifts from Lynesha and Emma to the image

on Ms. Jordan's right forearm — a tattoo of a bald eagle

with the American flag in the background.

Ms. Jordan sees me looking and pulls her sleeve down.

Again, she tells us that we will create poetry.

"That's better than reading about a bunch of dead guys

who you can't understand what they were writing about," says Ladarius.

"I didn't say that we would not learn about

some of the great poets of earlier centuries," Ms. Jordan replies.

"There is so much we can learn from their writings

about love, life, nature, and government.

                     Does anyone have any QUESTIONS?"

"Yeah. I heard you adopted a Black kid. Is that true?" says Lynesha.

Pressing her lips together and pausing before speaking,

        "My son is adopted. HE IS BLACK," says Ms. Jordan.

Fajah rakes her fingers over natural braids.

A menacing grin forms on her lips.

"Is that why you want to teach this class?" she asks,

"so you can learn how to parent a Black kid?"

"I like teaching, and I like poetry

as much as I hope you like learning," says Ms. Jordan.

Fajah's grin fades.

Tayvion stops tossing the basketball back and forth between his palms.

"That's all good," he says, "but what do you know about being Black?"

"What do you know about basketball?" Ms. Jordan asks.

"You can't be serious." Tayvion spins the ball on his finger.

"Everybody knows I dominate the court,

but obviously, you haven't heard the report.

I average thirty-two points a game. My left-handed jumper is insane.

Last season, I scored twenty-eight points, even with an ankle sprain."

"But what do you know about how basketball got started?"

"What that got to do with poetry?" Zaquaisha pins Ms. Jordan with her eyes.

"Easy Quay. My bruh got this," says Jamir.

"Some bored Black dudes got together,
nailed a bucket to a tree and started shooting hoops."
Tayvion flicks his wrist.
"That's not how it happened," says Ms. Jordan.
"So what did I miss?"
"Basketball was invented at Springfield College in 1891 by a grad student
named James Naismith as a class assignment," Ms. Jordan explains.
"And by the way, Naismith was White."
"No way a White dude invented basketball."
Tayvion lowers his head, embarrassed that he did not know
how the game he loves with all his heart had gotten its start.
"Yeah way." Ms. Jordan raises her brow. Her lips curve upward.
"If we can get past stereotypes, we might just learn
a few things about this literary form of art."

Emma leans forward in her wheelchair.
From my side view,
I can see Jasmine and Zaquaisha resisting the urge to stare.
"Who is your favorite poet?" Emma asks.
"Edgar Allan Poe," Ms. Jordan replies.
"Never heard of the guy." Jaquesha shrugs.

That doesn't surprise me.
Jaquesha's idea of recommended readings
are fashion magazines for teens.

"He was a White crazy dude."
Jamir makes a circling motion with his index finger.
Jaquesha appears confused, so Jamir says,
"A nineteenth-century *Tales from the Crypt* kind of poet."

"Cool. I like *Tales from the Crypt*."
Jaquesha nods
and looks around as if she's waiting for an applause
because she is open to reading works by Poe.

"I like Thoreau," says Emma.
"'My life has been the poem I would have writ.
But I could not both live and utter it.'"
"Who's Thoreau?" Jaquesha asks.
"Henry David Thoreau was —
never mind," says Jamir.
"Just stick with fashion magazines.
They're easier on your brain."
"What's that supposed to mean?" asks Jaquesha.
"What he's trying to tell you is stay in your lane,"
says Ladarius. "Fashion is your lane."

Jaquesha smiles when she hears the word fashion,
but Lynesha knows Jaquesha just got played,
so she says, "Girl everybody knows you're a fashionista.
Just look at you. Your hair. Your nails, and your clothes
are always on fleek.
When I win my first Grammy,
you're gon be my personal stylist,
and these scrubs gon be saying, 'I went to school with her.'
And we gon show them what it really means to be dissed."

Hadley raises her hand.
"Is this your first teaching assignment?" she asks.
"No," says Ms. Jordan.

Jasmine glances up from her cell phone.

"You look young. How long have you been teaching?" she asks.

"Long enough," Ms. Jordan answers.

Jasmine gives Ms. Jordan the stank face.

"Where you from?" Khalan asks.

Ms. Jordan holds her hands with her palms facing the class.

"Does anyone have any questions about your syllabus?"

"Yeah," I ask. "Can we write about anything we want to write about, or are you going to censor our writing?"

"This a creative writing class, so freedom of expression is expected.
You have the POWER OF CHOICE."

"That's good because I got to have freedom of expression," I say.

"Me too," says Fajah.

"She thinks she is another Amanda Gorman," Tayvion laughs.

Fajah cuts her eyes at him. "Boy, don't play with me," she says.

"As for censorship," Ms. Jordan continues,

"we will adhere to school policies.

Now let's begin with introductions.

Who wants to go first?"

"I'll go first," says Emma.

Emma's Truth

"As you can see, my legs don't work, but my brain functions just fine.
I can hear when people talk about me and see when people gawk at me.
It's not like I'm
DEAF OR BLIND.
They ask each other questions about how
I ended up in a wheelchair as they point and stare.
For the record, it was a car accident. It happened three years ago.
My parents were killed, and I lived.
I moved in with my aunt and uncle and their five kids.
They had another child, but she died of SIDS.
Living with them is not ideal, but it's better than foster care.
I have a roof over my head, and I'm safe there.
I have limited mobility in my left arm.
My aunt and uncle have been great at helping me
adjust to living with physical impairments.
They're nice. They're just not my parents."

Emma nods like she just told her truth.
She isn't asking for pity,
but her wheelchair is proof
that your
               LIFE CAN BE CHANGED IN AN INSTANT
by a tragedy.

———

DeAndre goes next.

Me, They, Him, Them

"Everybody in here knows my name is DeAndre.
I am the only male cheerleader
on the varsity cheerleading squad.
People spend more time questioning
my sexual identity
than getting to know me.
Most think I am a fraud because I don't identify
as gay or straight.
They ask what pronouns I prefer — he, him, they, them,
expecting me to bite the bait.
Would it make a difference if I told you I was queer?"
he asks, twirling a lock of his dreads
around his right pointer finger
before tucking his hair behind his ear.
His voice fluctuates from low and raspy to high pitch.
"When I began putting my thoughts down on paper," he adds,
"I realized that poetry is my niche,
so, when I heard about this class, I signed up for it."

Kabria—the Chameleon

I'm Kabria, best known as the mixed chick.
  I've learned a unique trick —
    how to maneuver between two worlds.
      I'm a CHAMELEON.
When I hang with my White friends,
  I THINK, ACT, AND TRY TO LOOK WHITE.
    When I hang out with my Black friends,
      I THINK, ACT, AND TRY TO LOOK BLACK.
        Some days I'M TOO WHITE
          and other days I'M TOO BLACK.
When I laugh or talk in a way that makes me feel comfortable,
  my WHITE FRIENDS say
    I'M TOO LOUD,
      that I need to tone it down.
        THOSE WORDS hang over my head
          LIKE A DARK CLOUD.
            When I tone it down, my BLACK FRIENDS say
              I'M TRYING TO SOUND WHITE.
                Their words are like a STARLESS NIGHT.
I get dissed for trying to FIT IN EITHER WORLD,
  like I'm BEING DISLOYAL if I hang out with one race
    more than the other. IT'S A LONELY PLACE.
      People define biracial people by their own biases.
      They make you THE CHAMELEON YOU BECOME.
        WORDS AND LOOKS as poisonous as venom.
          They judge you by skin tone, hair, and eye color.
          They judge you when you laugh, when you talk,
            by the way you walk.

They ask cruel questions, like whether
    I identify more with my White mother or my Black father,
  but not once has anyone asked
WHAT IT FEELS LIKE TO BE ME.

———

What it feels like to be me.
Maybe that is what this class is all about,
Maybe that's what poetry is about —
discovering what it means to be ourselves.

Call it an introduction or an icebreaker,
but this was much better than writing a paper
about what we hoped to learn in this course.
Talk about classroom diversity.
There is Black power and White supremacy,
multiracial ethnicity, a person with a physical disability,
White privilege and LGBT,
and a student whose family crossed the border illegally.
I know this because I heard him
telling the school counselor that his parents were undocumented.

We got anger, frustration, disappointments,
but we also got hopes and dreams,
maybe not MLK's dream of living in a nation
where we will not be judged by the color of our skin,
but we got dreams —
like rapping on the big stage,
singing at the Grammys,
playing in the NBA,

walking in the park,
creating fashions,
being accepted for who we are,
not having to be a chameleon just to fit in.

With verbal introductions out of the way,
we are given our first written assignment —
write a poem about current issues like how the pandemic
affected our mental health,
climate change, and immigration,
or whatever else was on our minds.
It didn't have to be about Black and White issues,
such as police brutality against Blacks
and racial disparities in education,
or other social ills that affect our nation.
              We were given the POWER OF CHOICE.

The next day Ms. Jordan greets us with a friendly, "Hello."
She's wired like her first cup of morning joe
had triple the caffeine.
We return muffled greetings.
She calls the roll and asks who wants to present first.
We complain, but she pulls up her syllabus
that states the entire classroom period will be utilized
for instruction. That's the sobering moment
when over half the class realizes
that this is not going to be an easy A.
There's no way that I'm not walking across that stage
and making my mama proud, so whatever I got to do to make the grade,
I gotta do what I gotta do.

"Why don't you go first, Ms. Jordan?" says Jamir.
"Yeah, show us what you got," says Tayvion.

No surprise that they teaming up.
Jamir is Tayvion's brother from another mother.
Tayvion has looked out for him ever since Jamir
got jumped for not gangbanging,
so you not gon see one without the other.
Tayvion got Jamir's back on the streets.
Jamir got Tayvion's back on the court.
Them dudes serious ballers,
like they came out the womb shooting hoops.
College scouts coming to their games.
NBA dream closer in view.
Jamir and Tayvion already picking out draft night suits.

Ms. Jordan's eyes crinkle. "Alright," she says.

Today

I reside between yesterday's disappointments and tomorrow's fears.
I have been with you throughout the years.
Though I am hardly visible as the focus is on what has already happened.
Or what could possibly be.

      Yesterday imprisons and tomorrow paralyzes,

      but today you have the opportunity to be free.

I watch you worry about what sorrows tomorrow may bring,
and what troubles yesterday brought.
However, today is counted as naught,
while you cry about yesterday and worry about tomorrow.
Though I plead with you to enjoy me,
you deny me time after time,
hoping to find comfort in tomorrow
when I offer you peace today.

      You have trust issues because you were hurt by yesterday;

      and therefore, dread tomorrow.

Much to my dismay my plea continues to fall on deaf ears.
Despite my best efforts, yesterday interferes
with today's happiness, and tomorrow's apprehensions
hover over today.
Perhaps you will come to the realization that

      today is here for you now,

      and when you do,

      I will be patiently waiting for you.

———

"That was tight," says Jamir.
Ms. Jordan smiles and says that she's glad her poem

meets his approval.

Now Jamir is the one tossing the basketball between hands.

He pauses and says that he thought a man

named Spalding created basketball.

Ms. Jordan reminds him that it's okay that he didn't know the answer.

Jamir says that he'd like to learn more about the history of the game.

Tayvion frowns, still embarrassed that as team captain he didn't know

the answer.

"It's all good, Tay," Jamir says, addressing his bruh by his nickname.

Jamarcus raises his hand to present next.

He pretends to be an average student,

but the dude is an Einstein.

I don't know if he does it to fit in

but it's not working for him.

One look at Jamarcus and the word "nerd" instantly comes to mind.

It takes more than a striped shirt, baggy cuff denims,

and a retro high top fade

to convince people that you're just average

when you love science as much as he does.

"I'll go next," says Jamarcus.

"So what do you want to share?" Ms. Jordan asks.

"Let's talk about this global warming stuff," he says.

Climate Change

It's getting hotter and the polar bear is STRUGGLING
to maintain as the ice caps melt away,
but you say let's reserve those discussions for another day.
I say when is that day gonna come,
when we, like the gray wolves, AIN'T GOT NO PLACE TO RUN,
when the ozone layer has been eaten away by the sun.
All so we can be COMFORTABLE down here.
Can't talk about it, or you say we spreading fear,
so, here's what we do:
Turn on our smart TVs, surf the Internet, grab a nice cold drink,
but we ain't giving up our conveniences 'cause we like how they make
us feel.
Hmph! But global warming ain't real,
which brings me to my next point — PLASTICS.
They are a part of the global warming problem too.
Paper bags were cool until back in the '60s,
when consumers decided to try something new.
It was exciting to think of their durability,
but what to do with them after we're done, we had no clue.
Someone came up with a plan.
We dug giant holes to dump our waste,
hoping to make it DISAPPEAR without a trace,
but it escapes,
releasing toxins in the soil that grows the food we eat
and float around in the air we breathe.
Marine animals are dying because they're ingesting plastics
that harm their digestive tracts.
That ain't fiction. I'm spitting real facts.

The ocean has become a landfill.

You still think THE PROBLEM ain't real?

RECYCLE — this goes here and that goes in that bin over there.

We recycle to ease our CONSCIENCE,

but not to save the planet

as we struggle to find a place for the plastic we DISCARD.

We manufacture MORE,

leaving our planet marred as we bombard

China who refuses to be the world's dumping ground

for recycled trashes,

so now they are not even tradable.

A FRAGILE ecosystem with plastics that are not biodegradable.

Tayvion's Turn

Ms. Jordan thanks Jamarcus for sharing his thoughts on climate change,
but his classmates are looking at him strange,
like what does this have to do with us?
No one appears to be interested in learning about science
in a poetry class. After a minute of silence,
Tayvion says that he is all for saving the planet,
but he wants to talk about something else,
meaning anything else.
He walks to the front of the room.
like a creepy undertaker,
his face crumpled like a prune.
Then he smiles a smile as big as the moon,
and says, "I am the face of depression.
I can wear a smile or a frown.
I can appear to be up when I'm feeling down.
I laugh. I cry,
and if you ask me to explain either emotion,
I could not tell you why.
I am depression."

Depression

Everybody's suffering from

D
  E
   P
  R
 E
S
 S
  I
   O
 N.

A
  reeling
    economy,
      global pandemic,
       cyberbullying,
        problems at home,
         problems on the job.
          Issues that no one CAN SOLVE.
                Turning to the bottle,
           turning to the pill,
         trying to stay grounded
      while climbing uphill,
    thinking a fix will do the trick.
    Uploading selfie pics.
  The more likes you get, the more you crave.

A selfie junkie.
A social media SLAVE.
Online all the time. Going live.
Everything from posting what you wear
to how you do your hair and what you eat.
Makes me wonder if you ever sleep.
Whatever happened to relaxing, reading a good book,
going for a morning jog.
Taking a little time to meditate.
You're depressed because you are gaining weight,
but you can find the time
to put your business online,
spilling the tea or trying to impress
everybody by your success.
Relationship lies,
the number one story we buy.
They look so happy. Got you looking at your partner
sideways 'cause you want what they got.
What you don't know is that their relationship is fake.
You only see what they want you to see.
It is like watching reality TV.
Depressed because of
lies posted online.
Ain't nobody that happy all the time.

——

"No cap," says Jamir.
Then he starts talking about the pressure to post selfies
to prove to your girl that you not cheating.
Lynesha and Jaquesha push back 'cause they both been played before.

They start naming playas that attend our school.
Zaquaisha sitting there taking notes like she's keeping score.
I ain't worried 'bout them calling my name.
I've never been a player.
Some of the guys can't say the same.
Zahair interrupts and says he wants to go next.
He's scared Jasmine gon spill the tea.
Zahair likes to catch and release.
He's dating Lynesha's cousin, Brittany,
and he always got a shawty on his side,
riding high during low tide.
But it's just a matter of time before he's busted.
Lies reconstructed
to sound like the truth.
But ain't no playa plan foolproof.

Zahair points his finger like a gun.

The Teller

He stared the teller in the eyes and demanded he hand over the cash.
The teller pushed the call button.
He shot him. Both lives CHANGED in a flash.
Doctors say the teller will never walk again
after taking a bullet to the neck.
My brother's lawyer says Rayshawn is lucky if he does twenty to life.
It's called CAUSE AND EFFECT.
Because the teller wouldn't give him money he had not earned,
now the teller's quality of life has CHANGED,
his children and his wife suffering,
but that's none of the robber's concern.
One moment of stupidity can cause a lifetime of PAIN.
A gun, a bad temper, and a bank robbery.
So many losses. Nothing gained.
Day after day, he reflects on his DECISION.
For anyone who thinks not carrying a gun makes you a punk,
consider spending the next twenty years in prison.

———

Zahair's brother robbed a bank over on Third Street.
He wrote this poem about him.
Then he shares how for an entire year,
he'd endured the agony of listening to his mother cry herself to sleep,
only to wake up to a nightmare.
"Life isn't always fair,"
he says. Zahair's right.
Life is all about cause and effect.
We are either a product of our doing or someone else's decision.

Emma McCarthy volunteers to go next.

Her parents were killed,

and she became paralyzed when their car was struck by a drunk driver.

Cause and effect.

The product of another person's decision.

Why Won't You Work?

Lazy, Good for Nothing!

That's what you are.
I hate it when you don't work.
I don't know why I even keep you around.

I Hate You!

Every time I look at you, I feel disgust.
I used to feel pity for you,
but not anymore.

You're Worthless!

I know I shouldn't say those things to you,
but that's how I feel.

I'm Embarrassed by Your Presence!

Why won't you work?
I know you can.
Don't you even want to try?

You're Stubborn!

But I can be stubborn too.
Sometimes I just don't understand you.
You always worked before,

and now you're willing to give up just like that.

It bothers me to see you in this state . . .
I don't know how to help you anymore.
Therapy seems to be a waste of time.
After the accident, you've been so uncooperative.

Some days I feel fortunate to have you around . . .
Other days I can't stand the sight of you.
I considered letting you go,
but my life would be incomplete without you.
We've been together so long.

I Really Don't Hate You . . .
I'm just angry because today I wanted
to go for a walk in the park,
but because you won't work,
I had to use this wheelchair instead.
As I watched others walk and jog,

I Got Angry with You!
I long to be able to do those things again.
Maybe someday you'll work
and I too will be able to go
for a jog in the park.

———

Jasmine crosses the color barrier line
and says at first, she thought Emma was talking about a disloyal friend,
who Jasmine was ready to defend

Emma against.

DeAndre admits he also thought Emma was talking about a friend.

For the first time, since the first day of class,

someone asks about style and form.

"Was that a simile or metaphor?" DeAndre asks.

"The term you are looking for is called personification,"

Ms. Jordan explains, "giving an object or an animal human characteristics.

In Emma's poem, she talks to her legs

as if they are a person with whom she is very frustrated."

"What is it called when a story is exaggerated?" says Kabria.

"Hyperbole," says Ms. Jordan.

Choices

Connor Fleming, the white guy dressed all Goth,
with spike cartilage earrings and lip, nose, and brow piercings,
says he's ready to share his poem.
You best believe all eyes are on him.
I don't know much about the Goth culture,
but dude looks like he needs to be
carrying a crow on his shoulder.
Connor walks to the front of the room.
Is it me, or did this room just get colder?

"Ms. Jordan, you said that in this class,
we have the power of choice, so I wrote about choices."
Connor threads his fingers through his hair.
Turns his chair
backwards and takes a seat.
With a crooked smile and furrowed brows,
and smoldering eyes like darkened clouds,
he recites his poem.

Hit and Run

Speeding
      down
          the
             highway
when he heard a loud thump.
Stopped
     and
        pulled
            over
wondering what he bumped.
Not
    another
        roadkill

      d
       e
        n
          t
           i
         n
        g
up
   his
      ride.

Seeing what he hit

        made

             him

                    sick

                           inside.

How could he not have seen him?
But then again, the man had on dark clothing,

                        and

                  it

             was

          a

     dark

night.
Maybe the man would have been more visible
had he worn something bright.
He

      tried

          calling

               for

                    help.

No cell phone service out here.
How could he explain that I only had one beer?

                           He

                    checked

             for

         vital

signs.
The guy was obviously dead.
There was nothing he could do for him.

A
    million
        thoughts
           ran
              through
                 his
                    head.
Should he put the body in the car
or leave it lying there.
Perplexed and in shock,

                      this
                  was fast
              becoming
            his
          worst
        nightmare.
Finally, after much debate,
he could no longer wait.
He fled the scene
and has regretted his decision
        then,
          now,
          and
            every
              day
               in
                 between.
He was not a monster or a cold-hearted soul,
just a scared young man
with high hopes and a goal

of becoming a doctor someday.
In an instant, how could he throw it all away?

A

        DUI,

                vehicular homicide.

                        No,

                              this

                                      was

                                      one

                              mistake

                      he

                had

        to

      hide.

Now he carries this dark secret everywhere he goes,
as dark as the night it happened,
as bitter as the frozen snow.

One

      drink.

          One

                night.

                      One

                            person

                                  dead.

Too many lives shattered. Too many regrets.
Too many memories playing inside his head.

A

reality.

A

nightmare.

He

can't

escape.

It follows him everywhere.

They say the truth will set you free,

but the truth would mean prison for me.

Am

I

speaking

fact

or

fiction?

You'll never get a conviction.

He'll swear to his innocence in a police interrogation,

that this story was only a fabrication

created by an overactive imagination.

The Witnesses

An awkward silence fills the room.
Connor has just lowered the boom.
Like castaways sending up SOS flares,
we wait for Ms. Jordan's response with fixed stares.
This dude had gone to the dark side
and had taken us along for the ride.
Ms. Jordan swallows hard.
"Who's next?" she asks,
as if she expects us to disregard
what we just heard.

Connor just proved what we had been saying all along.
This is the America in which we live, where a White boy
can stand in a room of twenty people and confess
to hit and run and not worry about catching a charge.
Students of color shouting he should go to jail,
demanding to know if his poem is fact or fiction,
teacher's rose-colored cheeks now pale.
We all waiting for Ms. Jordan to say something,
do something. Call the SRO to write a report.
What difference would it make?
We all know Goth boy is never gonna confess to committing a crime.
The police aren't going to do anything about it,
but if that was me or someone whose skin looked like mine,
they wouldn't hesitate to investigate.
As for Ms. Jordan, she inhales sharply,
says we are done sharing creative works for today
and that the remainder of the class period

will be spent learning poetic devices.
"We've already mentioned personification.
Does anyone have any more questions about personification?"
she asks.

I left the poetry class with MIXED FEELINGS.
I was all for freedom of expression,
but today I was certain that I had witnessed a confession.
Connor's words were more than just those of an overactive imagination.
They were detailed, as if he had firsthand knowledge of the situation.
He really should have exercised his Fifth Amendment right against
SELF-INCRIMINATION.
Walls talk, and it wouldn't be long before someone in poetry class
told someone outside of class
that Connor hit a pedestrian with his car and fled the scene,
but that someone wasn't going to be me.
I wasn't going to say or do anything
that would give administration a reason
to cancel the Black poetry class.

———

RACIAL TENSIONS in the city were rising.
Resulting in more protests and more candlelight vigils.
A police officer was seen in a video kicking a Black person
who was already on the ground in handcuffs.
The more videos surfaced, the more protesters took
their message of intolerance to the streets.
The protests went on for weeks.
Some were peaceful.
Others involved burning and looting.

Blacks were practically being stopped for sneezing in public.
We weren't the only ones feeling the heat,
so were Latinos, Asians,
and people whose origin was from the Middle East.
Freestyling and poetry class
is how I got through it. ALL OF IT.
Poetry class was more like a venting session.
Someone would read a poem, make a statement, or ask a question
that ended up in a full-blown discussion.
Discussion may not be the right word to use.
They were more like heated debates
with Ms. Jordan redirecting us,
but she couldn't seem to get around that
ELEPHANT IN THE ROOM.

ACT 2

Imitation of Black

Rumor has it that Ms. Jordan is a trust fund baby.
Rumor also has it that Ms. Jordan moved to the Black side of town,
so her Black adopted child could grow up around his people
and that her husband was willing to go along with her adopting a
Black child,
but when she decided to move to the hood, he bailed.
I can't say that I blame him.
Most Blacks wanna move out of the hood,
but Ms. Jordan moving in?
Maybe she's EXPERIENCING WHITE GUILT.
I read a book about it.
White people feeling guilty for slavery,
and all the privileges they got
at the expense of my peoples' suffering,
so, they try to right a wrong
by sacrificing themselves.
They try desperately to relate to us.
They want to know WHAT IT FEELS LIKE TO BE BLACK,
and when they can't, they come as close it as possible,
like moving into a Black neighborhood and eating fried chicken
and collard greens at some hole-in-the-wall place.

No Justice! No Peace!

Every day in the Black poetry class,
we were tackling tough issues,
the kind that make you keep a box of tissues,
if you're a bleeding heart, that is,
or angry enough to clench your fist.
IT IS WHAT IT IS.
Not looking for sympathy
but I need you to notice me,
to acknowledge that I exist,
that my pain is real,
that my voice is not an empty drum
and that my past is not the sum
total of who I am,
but it is also not something to be ignored
or dismissed.
Respect is a right not a wish.
I AM IN THIS BLACK SKIN.
That's not going to change.
What has to change is the way you see me.
I'm a person not a thing.
If you try to figure me out,
I will keep you guessing.
Too many assumptions.
What's wrong with conversing?
That's the problem between the Black community and the police.
We want to speak our piece,
and they want us to hold our peace.
NO JUSTICE! NO PEACE!

That's the message we are sending,
but the violence against us isn't ending.
We are told to be patient.
Meanwhile,
our mamas got the undertaker on speed dial.

Jamir mentions that the police shot another unarmed Black man.
He survived the shooting, but the whole left side of his face is gone.
DeAndre wants to know what Ms. Jordan has to say about the shooting.
Caroline and Hunter want to know her views on the burning and looting.

"I think we need to go ahead and get started on today's lesson,"
says Ms. Jordan.
"Okay, then I want to share my thoughts on the criminal justice
system in this country," says DeAndre.
Ms. Jordan pastes on a polite smile,
but DeAndre isn't smiling,
not even a fake one.
There's nothing to smile about when you wake up
to hear about an unarmed bruh in CCU,
and a badge, a bullet, and a gun.
"Obsolete," says DeAndre.

Obsolete

You told me I was OBSOLETE
when I cried for equality, and you turned a deaf ear.
You told me I was obsolete
when petty crimes I committed were esteemed severe.
You told me I was OBSOLETE
when I received the maximum sentence
punishable by law,
and you turned me over to a penal system
worse than the devil's claw.
You told me I was OBSOLETE
when perpetrators that commit crimes against me
are free to do it again.
You told me I was OBSOLETE
when I was first in line
but was placed on a waiting list.
You told me I was OBSOLETE
when I was forced to adhere
to rules and laws that only applied to my kind.
You told me I was obsolete when justice was blind.
You told me I was OBSOLETE
when a tall darker complexion man
is confused with a short lighter complexion one,
in a lineup because in your eyes we all look the same.
You told me I was OBSOLETE
when I was made to bear the shame
of having to take a backseat
when I earned first chair.
You told me I was OBSOLETE

when I worked hard but was never given
my fair share.
You told me I was OBSOLETE,
but that was far from the truth.
My resilience is like a fountain of youth.
You told me I was OBSOLETE,
by your attitude and words that offend,
but I will rise above it all time and time again.
You could never understand what it means to be me
when Black is all other people see.
You could never understand
what it means to be treated LESS THAN A MAN
and you're expected to win
when in reality you lost the fight before it began.
You could never imagine
how it feels
when sales associates follow you around in stores
waiting for you to steal
so they can call a trigger-happy cop
who commands you to stop
doing something you weren't doing in the first place
and he arrests you because of your race.
You could never grasp
the disappointment of
always coming in last
or comprehend
the tears suppressed by a grin.
And you feel the need to prove your INNOCENCE
while the boys in blue claim self-defense
and are dealt no real consequence

and you wonder why Blacks are so skeptical.
It's because the US criminal justice system is UNACCEPTABLE.

———

Jamir replies that our country treats us
the way they see us,
the same way they saw our ancestors,
as people to be brutalized.
Caroline takes offense to America being criticized
for how she has historically treated people of color
and says she has no White guilt
for what we say happened to our ancestors.
What does she mean by 'what you say happened.'
We all know it happened.
Connor joins the conversation
and says he's tired of hearing about slavery
and that we should appreciate our founders' bravery
to come to an untamed territory
and make it the great country it is today.
Jamir tells him to shut up MAGA boy.
Connor mouths something that sounds like the N-word.
Jamir clenches his fist and leaps from his seat.
I jump to my feet and say, "No White guilt."
I'm not the only one who needs this class to graduate.
"Don't do it. You're going to get kicked out of school,"
I whisper only loud enough for Jamir to hear.
Jamir unclenches his fist and takes his seat as I take the floor.

No White Guilt

No White guilt,
you say.
I'm not responsible for the blood my ancestors spilled.
But if I receive stolen property
from someone found guilty of committing a theft crime,
I'd end up doing time.
WHY SHOULD YOU BE ANY DIFFERENT?
Everything your people got was stolen through slave labor
and the Indian Removal Act,
but you don't want to face the fact
that you have profited from the suffering
of my people and that of Native Americans,
but I won't hold you accountable
FOR THE DECISIONS YOUR ANCESTORS MADE.
Only for trying to rewrite history to free them from blame.
Your forefathers came to America and built a great nation.
For that they get a standing ovation
along with the African slaves who carried the heavy load,
the Chinese who built the transcontinental railroad,
and the Indians who taught the settlers
how to turn woodlands into farmlands.
It's true your forefathers grew America into a great nation
but not without getting BLOOD ON THEIR HANDS.
The Africans were chained and beaten with whips.
The Chinese suffered unspeakable woes.
The Indians who saved the first settlers from starvation
were treated like foes.
THE TRUTH ABOUT AMERICAN HISTORY has yet to be told

because you are afraid of White guilt.

But for us, American history has never been about White guilt.

It's about the conscience of a nation,

cycles of oppression, a continuous rotation.

   LEARNING FROM THE PAST, NOT FORGETTING IT.

Periodt!

———

Jamir raises his hand like a bidder at an auction.

"I want to go next," he says.

Ms. Jordan nods, giving him the go-ahead.

Real Talk

It was just ANOTHER DAY on Ferguson Street
shooting hoops with my homies
when Taeshon Phillips landed at my feet.
He had taken A STRAY BULLET to the head,
and just like that dude was dead.
I had known Tae since the age of ten.
He was MORE THAN a brother of color.
He was my best friend.

I didn't see the shooter.
The car was moving way too fast.
One gun. One bullet. One blast.
One year has passed.
His life cut too short. Mine FOREVER CHANGED.
The memories still fresh.
The bullet went into his head,
and THE PAIN ripped through my chest.
I fell to my knees and cradled him in my arms,
sobbing like a baby. Someone call 911,
I screamed. This crap was real. NO FALSE ALARM.
Strangers surrounded us like a swarm of bees
until blaring sirens in the distance were heard,
and these imposters fled like prison escapees.

But my bro was down for the count.
I had A CHOICE. I could stay or bounce.
The police were questioning me as if I did something wrong.
What about MY GRIEF, my pain?

Never mind what I had just undergone.

Bruhs ain't got no feelings, right?
'Cause we all thugs, hustlers, doing and selling drugs, women beaters.
That's what you think.
That's how we are PORTRAYED BY THE MEDIA.
Always got to prove ourselves.
Forced to hold in our pain until we EXPLODE.
Proving you right all along.
A no-win situation. MISINFORMATION.

That we don't care about OUR COMMUNITIES.
Spare me the rhetoric please.
We've heard it all before.
No more.
My generation, much like my ancestors,
is tired of the same old conversation.
We need opportunities to better our communities
and to be viewed as people, not lethal weapons.
PERCEPTIONS.
MISCONCEPTIONS.
And so we buy into the lie
that brothers from the hood only had two options:
DEATH OR PRISON.
Just another bruh off the street,
But I want you to know HIS LIFE MATTERED,
To me, his family, his community.
When he died, our lives were SHATTERED.
But I can't allow my homie to be forgotten.
He was my bruh. He was MY FRIEND.

He wasn't doing anything wrong.
Just hoops with the guys
when his life came to a TRAGIC END.

So remember that THE NEXT TIME you see one of us
and think thug from the hood,
up to no good,
or you have an urge to call the police
on an unwarranted suspicion
that could land an INNOCENT brother in prison.
We don't need a statistician
reminding us that we populate the penal system.
What we need is for you to join us
in our fight to save OUR GENERATION from eradication.
Real Talk.

———

That's as real as it gets, but Jackson Chandler didn't get the memo.
He wants to impress Hunter.
Jackson is what some people call PWT
(Poor White Trash). I just call him a wannabe.
Jackson has as much of a chance fitting in with Connor and his friends
as Meghan Markle has of fitting in the British royal family.

"Why is it that your people keep killing one another
and complain about gun violence," says Jackson.
"Bro, he just gave you a demo
of what life is like for young bruhs every day," says Tayvion.
"This is real life. This ain't no screenplay.
Walk a mile in my shoes,

then you'll clearly understand a Black man's blues."

"Black girls got blues too," says Fajah.
"We got blues 'cause we got dreams.
Don't you know colored girls aren't allowed to dream?"
she says, changing her voice to a 1950s deep Southern accent.
"We's supposed to cook and clean for other folks that got dreams.
I've been told that I'm silly for dreaming.
But I do it anyhow. I guess I never learned the meaning
of a colored girl's reason for being
'cause I ain't got no desire to be a maid or a cook.
If you're looking for me and can't find me,
well, you'll find my head in a book."

Silly Girl

Silly girl, who told you that dreams were
For little dark girls like you?
With your nappy hair and thick lips
Everyone knows
Those are not pretty girls' looks.
Silly girl, what are you holding in your arms?
That had better not be books.
Silly girl practicing the way you speak,
Learning all those big, fancy words,
Trying not to break verbs.

Silly girl with pipe dreams
And hopes of going to college,
Swelling with pride
Because of all that head knowledge.

Silly girl, what's that in your hand,
An application for scholarships, once again?
Where do you think you're going
With your dark skin,
Nappy hair, and thick lips?
Silly girl, just because you graduated from college
With all those tassels and things
Hanging around your neck,
Don't think you're some kind of big success.

Silly girl, I heard you won
The Nobel Peace Prize.

You help to change the world,
But ain't done a thing to change our lives.
To us you're nothing but a silly girl,
Always was and always will be.
Don't think that we're impressed
'Cause you some big success.
We don't need books and college,
Pipe dreams and head knowledge.
Nothing wrong with the way we think and talk.
We ain't never gonna change.

So, you go on silly girl with your dark skin,
Nappy hair and thick lips and make us proud of you.
We always was and always will be.

——

"Why they clowning her like that?" Jasmine rolls her neck.
"Girl, they not clowning her," says Lynesha. "They trying to protect
her from hurt and disappointment, right, Fajah?"
Fajah tells Lynesha that her interpretation of her poem was on point.
Caroline blurts something about Black people passing for White
during slavery as if that somehow relates to Fajah's poem.
I think she only wants a participation grade.
Her comments succeed in sparking a debate
about passing.
Zaquaisha not about to let that go without a challenge,
so she says what about the White woman
who was the head of the NAACP chapter
in Spokane, Washington.
Caroline whips her head around like somebody slapped her.

Racial Passing

What a startling claim,
  a White person among you
    pretending to be Black.
      Not an ounce of Black blood anywhere to be found.
        REVERSE PASSING.
          Light-skinned Blacks passing as White to escape racial hate.
        Now dark-skinned White people passing as Black for what reason?
Do you think poverty is a racial privilege?
Do you identify as Black to relate to our struggle of racism and
inequality?
Time spent in a tanning bed and curly hair or braids on your head
won't make you Black and that's a fact.
We were BORN BLACK inside and out.
No doubt.
We didn't wake up with a revelation
and make a radical transformation.
We have lived the struggle and all that comes
along with being born Black,
  but you MISREPRESENT our race.
    Thinking the changes you made
      somehow make you Black.
        There is so much more you lack.
          The BLACK STRUGGLE is REAL.
            Being BLACK is not an act.
              Collecting public assistance from the state
              when you didn't need it,
          was that so you could feel that poverty was real?
        Are you CONVENIENTLY BLACK?

Do you shed it like an overcoat?
Do you watch Blacks and take notes?
Whites masquerading as Blacks.
Were you confused, or was this a ruse?
Our trust you abused.
We despise the lies you told.
YOU'RE NOT ONE OF US.
Never were. Never will be.
You are a fraud, hindering the cause.
Call it reverse passing or transracial identity.
It's all still fraud to me.

Wannabe

Hadley Hayes, the White girl who hangs
around Black people, claims
she can identify with our pain
because people diss her for acting Black.
She says it's not an act,
that she has embraced the Black culture.
She's proud she likes cornbread, candied yams, and black-eyed peas
and that her White friends treat her like she has a bad disease.
I hate when White people say they understand
what it feels like to be Black because they have Black friends.
That's an insult to our struggle for equality.
Saying you can identify with my pain is hypocrisy
because you're not forced to think about
the color of your skin every day
like it's a menacing thing instead a part of your being.

Judged by the Skin I'm In

If I go into a store, I am constantly asked by customer sales associates
if I need help, not that they are that eager to assist me,
but it is a subtle way to watch me without appearing too suspicious.
There are times when I ignore that the sales associate
always appears to be on the same aisle as I am or one aisle over.
Then there are times when it really bugs me that I AM BEING
WATCHED
when White customers shop freely without being policed.
During those times, I tell the sales associate
that they are free to do something else or help another customer
because I did not come to steal any items,
I came to purchase them.
Of course, they deny the obvious: that they had pegged me
as a shoplifter BECAUSE I AM BLACK.
I have had sales associates become irate with me
although I remained calm because no one wants
to be accused of being racially biased even when they are
PROFILING ME.

Javier Mendez, who's done more observation than participation,
says he wants to talk about what it feels like
when people just want you to go away,
when they wish they could make you disappear without a trace.

Undocumented

UNDOCUMENTED

Deportation

Separation

Alienation

Isolation

Border wall

Build it tall

Keep them out

Illegals

Illegal aliens

Illegal immigrants

Non-citizens

UNDOCUMENTED

Without status

Depression

Anxiety

Social isolation

Kids in cages

Twelve million

UNDOCUMENTED

Persons

Adults

Children

Families

DACA

Dreamers

Schemers

Illegal border crossings

Violent

Terrorists

Protect American jobs

Immigration

Violation

Recommendation

Deportation

UNDOCUMENTED.

———

Javier's poem leads to a debate over the border and immigration.
While some students argue that undocumented people broke
immigration laws,
others say they should have an opportunity for citizenship
since they are already here.
While other students' positions are unclear.

Hunter wants to send them back to their country.
Of course, he would. That's how the Extremes think.
They believe this is their country,
and that other races should be extinct.

"It's a good thing the Native Americans didn't feel that way,
or the first settlers would have starved to death."
Khalan tells Hunter that the settlers were immigrants
who came to America and killed the Indians who tried
to help them and drove the rest off of their land.
"And you know this firsthand,
or are you buying into a phony narrative of history?"
Hunter says White people did not steal the land from Indians

because they were nomadic and never settled in one place.
They fought the Indians who tried to reclaim the land
after White people made better use of it.
There are arguments about the harsh treatment of Haitians
in comparison to the treatment of Hispanics.
Hunter says aggressive enforcement is necessary
to avoid overpopulation and that Mexicans and Haitians
aren't the only problem, that terrorist Muslims are entering the country.
He says that's why we need a border wall
to keep out all the criminals.
Hadley counteracts with the words inscribed on the Statue of Liberty.

> Give me your tired, your poor,
> Your huddled masses yearning to breathe free,
> The wretched refuse of your teeming shore.
> Send these, the homeless, tempest-tossed to me:
> I lift my lamp beside the golden door!

Hunter says those words weren't meant for terrorists and rapists.
Kabria says that Hunter is a racist,
and she has heard that kind of talk at home from her parents.

Zaquaisha goes next. Her poem is about an enslaved African girl
reminiscing about her homeland.

I Long for Home

I long for home.
　　　I long for Africa
　　　　　where I am free to roam
　　　　　　　as I please, swing from vines,
　　　　　　　　climb banana trees.
I long to behold
　　　the beautiful color scheme —
　　　　　orange sunsets,
　　　　　　forests of green,
　　　　　　　sandy white beaches,
　　　　　　　waters so blue,
　　　　　　　zebra stripes, giraffe patches,
　　　　　　　gorillas chewing bamboo,
　　　　　　　ebony bodies swaying to the beat
　　　　　of sounding drums,
　　　　refreshing rains,
　　　relief from sweltering heat.
My mama's face I miss the most
　　　since the time I was stolen from the Ivory Coast.
　　　　　Will the soles of my feet
　　　　　　ever walk again upon the red earth?
　　　　　　　Upon thine shores I long to be.
　　　　　　　　How I long for thee, oh Africa.

———

Jasmine says the poem makes her want to cry
and that one day she'd like to visit Africa.
I'd like to visit Africa someday myself.

Caroline wants to know why
Black poetry is always about pain,
and why we can't write about something else.
Imagine walking barefoot with a thorn in your heel.
Would you notice the graceful stature of a lily in the field?

The Thorn in My Heel

THERE IS BEAUTY.
Most of the time, that beauty is hiding the pain
we feel on the inside.
See, we got real good at masking our pain,
but sometimes you get tired of the mask,
and you don't care who sees your pain.
THERE IS PAIN.
You just want to let it all out — the pain, the anger, the hurt,
the disappointment, the fear.
It's all real, but if you'd rather hear poems about roses,
just know that there are thorns among roses.
No matter how pretty the roses are,
THORNS HURT.
Sometimes those thorns are in my heels.
If you want to hear about beautiful daffodils,
and amazing sunsets
and rolling hills,
just remember those daffodils
might be on the unmarked grave of a slave,
or those sunsets
might be what I
CHOOSE TO REMEMBER
when I'm upset by news of another police shooting,
and those rolling hills
might be how I feel
caught in transition,
hopeful that things are changing
when I discover that more laws are being passed

to keep me as a second-class
citizen,
and I must make a decision
whether to allow anger to control me
or find a way to hide
THE PAIN AND MISERY
behind the beauty you want to see.

The Elephant in the Room

All eyes are on me
as I sum up my thoughts on the pain behind the beauty.
Ms. Jordan is watching me too.
It's hard not to talk about the elephant in the room.
It's like trying to ignore a sonic boom.
I like Ms. Jordan, and I appreciate what she is trying to do
by easing us into writing poetry about Black topics.
It's impossible to avoid conflicts.
You just can't overlook the obvious,
when Black and White issues are what we face every day.
News flash. We have a White supremacist in our class.
I don't know if Ms. Jordan gets it.
Hunter is not there for the credit.
No. He has something else in mind,
like antagonizing the Black students,
get us to respond with violence,
so the school board will be forced
to stop offering the course,
but the pen is mightier than the sword,
and since none of us seniors can afford
to fail this class, we're going to have to learn how
to deal with Hunter's racist comments
by applying restraint and common sense,
remaining calm when moments get tense.
It is easy to retaliate when your buttons are pushed,
and you react defensively when you're ambushed.
But "knowing is half the battle."
Since I know how the game is played,

I'm not about to allow him to rattle my cage.
Ms. Jordan dismisses our class.
We go our separate ways.
I'm off to gym, which is great
because I get to work off steam.
After dealing with Hunter, it's just what I need.
I survive the rest of the day
creating lyrics for my next battle with Jontrae.
Kaesan, Jay D, and Sultan come over after school.
Castille and Frederick show up too.
My mama is in the kitchen making her favorite beef stew.
We freestyling. Errbody smiling.
Popping lyrics like we are in a drop-the-mic competition.
We hitting the mark with precision,
only we not clowning each other.
Just rapping about life.
Errbody cool until I start rapping about color.
That's when Frederick goes all in,
like he's trying to resurrect the Black Panther Party.
Jay D ends, passing the mic with rapping about taking a knee.

Mama hollers from the kitchen,
"You boys ready to eat?"
She doesn't have to ask twice.
There's some things I'm going to miss about Dickerson
after graduation, but school lunch ain't one of them.

A Live Dog

Dinner time is spill-the-tea time.
My bruhs all want to know about the Black poetry class.
I tell them it's straight except for the White supremacist
who is trying to make me catch a charge,
but nothing is going to stop me from
getting my diploma.
Sultan isn't persuaded that I can keep my cool an entire semester.
Our less than heated debate is interrupted by the savory aroma
of Mama's beef stew.
Mama blesses the food, and we eat like it's our last meal
as we continue to spill
the tea on what's happening in the school and community.
Jay D wants to talk about the time capsule.
Kaesan says he's putting a picture of Shay Thompson in it
so that everyone can know what the prettiest girl
at Dickerson High School looked like fifty years earlier.
Of all the things he could put in a time capsule,
Kaesan wants to put in a picture of a girl he never dated.
Frederick says time capsules are overrated
and that a half century from now,
no one is going to care about what we wore
and what music we played,
or how we spent our days
talking, texting, and taking selfies.
Jay D suggests that we put in some BLM stuff
to let the future generation know about all these police killings
of unarmed Blacks.
Castille says that ain't necessary because fifty years from now,

nothing will have changed.

There will still be marches and protests for justice
and people trying to silence us.

Kaesan says he heard that some White boys
who call themselves The Extremes are planning on causing
trouble at the BLM protest Saturday.

Sultan says that the police are going to be there,
but it will probably be a repeat of Kenosha, Wisconsin,
with police handing out bottles of water
to dangerous militants
and arresting BLM protesters.

Castille says his cousin, Tyrell, got stopped by the police
for a broken taillight and ended up in a chokehold.

He survived the assault but says if there's ever a next time,
that officer won't live to tell the story.

"What's that supposed to mean?" I ask.

Castille smirks and says the next officer had better take inventory
before he stops Tyrell because now
he's packing AR-15 style.

"Death before dishonor," says Frederick.

"Nonsense," says Mama. "If an officer stops you, comply.

The Black community has already given the undertakers enough business.

We don't need to give mamas any more reasons to cry.

Besides, a live dog is better than a dead lion any day."

I Ain't About That Life

The city has been in an uproar since the Black pizza driver got shot,
Black dudes either afraid to leave their home,
or they go out looking to right a wrong.
I ain't afraid, but I know where a confrontation
with the police leads —
to the morgue or a jail cell,
and the boys in blue got the keys.
Mama always says, *"Keep your nose clean."*
I know exactly what she means.
I ain't about to give up on my dreams.
Easy money ain't nothing but trouble,
but since I don't live in a bubble,
I can't pretend that I don't know about the hustle.
I just focus on doing my thing.
Creating beats and rapping.
That's what you can find me doing most of the time.
I ain't about a life of crime.
Yeah you got some bad dudes out here creating mayhem,
but don't judge me because of them.
I ain't out here hustling,
so let me do my thing.

Race Riot

Me and my boys in the school caf doing what we do
when Nimrod and his crew
start spitting lyrics like we do in a battle rap.
I ain't got no other choice but to show him what I got,
so I start dropping the mic on the spot.
While I'm roasting him like I did in my dream,
somebody lets out a scream.
Two boys fighting in the hall.
One White, the other Mexican.
It all started because the White boy says
he can't wait until they finish building the wall
to keep Mexis out,
then he says he wants to send all Blacks
back to Africa, so this Black dude starts swinging.
The bell's ringing but ain't nobody trying to go to class.
White boy committed the ultimate trespass.
Black students pounding him
for telling them that they don't belong in the only country
they know as home.
A group of White boys come to the rescue.
I'm not liking the view,
but I stand back because I can't get kicked out of school.
Even though I ain't down with the way the White dude dissed
my race,
I got to think with my head, not my fist,
so I shove my hands into my pockets.
The area outside the cafeteria is filling up fast
with onlookers, but I walk past

them as I make my way to class.
Principal Martin shows up. Students scatter.
Once again, the halls are quiet.
Social media is calling the fight a race riot.
Some people are confused
because the evening news
suggests that Black Lives Matter
may be the cause of racial tensions at the school.
Mama calls it another attack on BLM to distract
attention from the real problem, which is cops killing Blacks.
A public nuisance is how the press likes to portray the organization.
Violent instigators when we are not the haters.
We are the ones being hated.
Negative publicity is what sells.
Reporters don't mind leaving out details,
like who started the so-called "race riot."

In poetry class, the racial divide widens.
Like blue states, red states, Trump's supporters, and Biden's.
The elephant in the room has just gotten bigger,
which means it's time for Ms. Jordan to consider
that you can't teach a Black poetry class
and ignore the fact that we are Black.
Countee Cullen, Rita Dove, and Langston Hughes
all refused to be silenced by criticism and racism.
They weren't afraid to write poetry about the issues
that plague communities throughout our nation.
We are all feeling the frustration of being expected to say
and do what is politically correct,
but that means having to neglect

our true thoughts and feelings,
which only leads to more discord and strife.
The tension is so thick, you could cut it with a knife.
I have to say something.

"Ms. Jordan, you're going about this all wrong.
You want to hand us a neatly wrapped present
filled with dog poop while you follow behind with a scoop
cleaning up after us.
I know you took your time, making the package all pretty
for the eyes to behold.
I am not attempting to scold
you for what you've done.
This school needed a course that would allow us
to be honest about the issues that plague our city.
Your packaging is pretty;
however, we can still smell what's inside the box and it stinks.
There is no way to get rid of that smell.
You can't spray perfume over it; that's what you've been trying to do.
We got to be free to express how we feel,
in a nonviolent manner, of course.
Sometimes we may get loud or angry.
There may be heated debates because the contents of the box stink,
but we got to let it out, and you got to let us do it.
We ain't gonna fight, at least not with our fists.
We gonna do what we came in here to do,
and that is write about what makes Black poetry our story.
Whether it is a tale of slavery or a police shooting,
we have a right to tell our story, to use our imaginations,
to use what we've seen, heard, and learned

to create Black poetry that will resound with messages

of beauty and pain,

satisfaction and disappointment,

triumph as well as tragedy

because that is what makes us who we are."

Ms. Jordan nods and asks if I'm ready to share my poem with the class.

Bloody Sunday

Tear gas, billy clubs, water hoses,
and canine teeth.
The world watched in disbelief
as the fury of racism was unleashed
upon men, women, and children of color,
a day that has gone down in history
unlike any other.
Bloody Sunday, as it has come to be known.
Oh, how the world bemoaned the cruelty shown
revealing hearts of stone.
Fed up with injustices and laws that promoted
inequality, peaceful demonstrators marched in protest.
Nonetheless,
they were confronted by Alabama State troopers
and Selma police, beaten mercilessly and then placed
under arrest.
As the world took notice,
the ill-treatment of people of color became the focus.
Blood spilled on Bloody Sunday was not in vain,
for others felt the Black man's pain
and expressed empathy for the growing antipathy
toward Blacks
and the agony they experienced on Bloody Sunday,
a day that will forever live in infamy.

———

I am glad for the chance to tell
the story of my people's ongoing battle

with racist attitudes and policies that fueled
systemic racism,
so, it stands to reason
that I struggled
to keep from losing it when Hunter Abbott chuckled
as if centuries of oppression were a joke.
That smug look — an almost successful attempt to provoke
me to respond with violence.
I am seeing red
and as much as I want to go upside his head,
I can hear my mama's voice saying,
Cooler heads prevail
and when they don't there are only two places
you land, and that's the grave or jail.
I have no desire to be in either place,
so, I keep my cool.
I got places to go and dreams to dream.
I got lyrics to write and beats to create.
In this business it's not enough to be good.
You gotta be great
or nobody's gon remember your name.
When you're going up against guys like Nimrod
you gotta bring your A-game.
That's what we been tryna do:
make a name for ourselves among the great artists
like Jay-Z and the the Notorious B.I.G.,
Lil' Kim and Eminem,
Tupac and Lil Wayne,
Missy Elliott and Lauryn Hill.
They had skills, but they had determination too.

That's what it takes to make it as a rapper.
So I'm determined to do what I got to do.
I wasn't sure what went down with my bruhs after I left,
but only one member of the crew
is waiting for me after school.
Kaesan says he doesn't know what happened to Castille and Sultan,
only that he heard they took Frederick downtown.
"That's really messed up," I say.

> "I started to jump in and HELP THE BRUHS OUT,"

he says, "but your mama's words kept playing in my head like a bad tune."
Mama always says, *No one is immune to trouble,*
but you just got to know how to respond when trouble finds you.
Kaesan says Jay D and Sultan were not involved in the brawl,
but he saw Castille punching a guy.

"Hi, Mason." Diamond waves as she passes me in the hall.
"Hey, girl. What's up?" I ask.

> *She smiles and KEEPS IT MOVING.*

Kaesan is checking out the girl walking with Diamond,
which has me wondering what happened between him and Cassidy.
He shrugs and says that he ain't into her like that
and that he's thinking about the two of them just being friends.
I know Kaesan likes Cassidy, but he worried about what people saying.
"Tsk. It is not what people are saying.

> *IT'S WHAT MY EYES ARE SEEING," he says.*

"She ain't ugly," I say. "She just needs a little TLC.
Some girls are like classic cars.
They need a wax job to bring out the shine."
"The glasses gotta go," he says. "If she gonna be with me,
she gotta wear contacts and get rid of that nineties hairstyle,

or we both WASTING OUR TIME."

"You can't expect her to change just like that.

Maybe she could use a makeover

and maybe she likes the way she looks.

You have a choice; you can tell her how you feel

and risk losing her, or you can tell her it's over and lose her."

"The glasses aren't that bad," Kaesan laughs,

"but that nineties hairstyle still got to go."

"Compromise. Don't criticize,"

I say, extending Kaesan a fist pump.

"Aight." Kaesan nods,

then asks, "When you and Nimrod gonna battle rap?"

"I ain't got time for that clown," I say.

I'm concerned about Castille and Frederick.

First offense probably a misdemeanor.

Most likely probation, but what about graduation?

Kaesan says ain't nothing we can do about their situation,

but let them know they still a part of the crew.

I want to go home and wait for news,

but Kaesan wants to go to Pendleton Park.

He's hoping Nimrod is gonna be at the park.

I call up Jay D and Sultan and tell them to meet us there.

Proving Ground

Anyone who wants to be a rapper
and lives within twenty miles of Pendleton
knows about Pendleton Park.
It's the place where legends are born
and raw talent is discovered.
A place where reputations are lost and recovered.
It is a training ground
and a proving ground.
When we arrive, Hitman is there.
Don't ask me how he got his rapper name.
I don't know, and I ain't sure I want to know,
but what I do know is that the dude got a crazy flow.
I accept his challenge
and leave him reeling,
wondering if he is on the floor or the ceiling.
Jay D and Sultan are on their game.
We put Hitman and his crew to shame.

One of Them

Walking home all excited.
Our passions reignited.
We had just held our own
freestyling with Hitman and his crew,
making it do what it do
when a patrol car pulls over
and an officer — whose name badge reads Hyatt —
begins questioning us about the school riot
and shouting commands like, "Show me your hands."

"You're one of the kids involved in the school riot."
I shake my head.
"Don't deny it.
I saw you on the video."
"I was there," I explain, "but I didn't fight 'em.
I didn't throw one single blow.
I went to class."
"You are lying," he says.
"He's telling the truth," says Jay D.

"Shut up before I lock you up for hindering
a police investigation," scolds Officer Hyatt.
"I'm not lying. I had nothing to do with the riot,"
I maintain my innocence,
but nothing I say makes a difference.
I don't want either of us to be tomorrow's hashtag,
so I plead with Jay D to keep his cool.
Officer Hyatt aims a gun at my head,

the moment every Black person dreads.
I want to bolt, but I stand still instead.
I close my eyes because I know I'm as good as dead.

"What's in your pocket?" he shouts.
"My keys," I reply.
"What did you do with the knife?"
"I don't have a knife."
I reach in my pocket to retrieve my keys.
"Keep your hands in the air, or I will blow
your freaking head off," he screams.
I raise my hands and drop my keys.
He sizes me up with his eyes.

"I heard about you. You're that rapper
who's always talking about how the cops
are the bad guys.
Nothing but a pile of lies
to discredit the uniform, the badge, and everything we stand for.
We keep law and order,
but you're some kind of rapper warrior.
A Tupac-Huey-Newton crossbreed, I suppose.
Just keep in mind the paths they chose
led to untimely deaths,
but you think they're heroes,
want to follow in their footsteps.
Just remember, we are the good guys."

My hands shake.
I tell him that he is making a mistake.

He brandishes his gun.

I'm too afraid to wait around for what happens next

and too afraid to run.

"Okay. Whatever you say. Just don't shoot."

I raise my hands high above my head

to show that I'm no threat,

but he's not done yet.

"I saw the riot tape. You were one of the instigators."

"Whatever?" I shrug.

"You did it," he repeats in a gravelly voice.

"You keep saying that I did it,

so obviously, you are persuaded I did it."

"You broke a guy's jawbone."

"I broke a guy's jawbone?" I scoff.

He flips the script.

"I'm placing you under arrest."

"What?"

"You just confessed

to inciting a riot," he says, grabbing my hands,

placing them behind my back,

and slapping on handcuffs.

"You can't be serious." I struggle to free my hands.

That's when it happens.

He throws me to the ground

face down.

A crowd gathers.

Another officer arrives on the scene.

"Don't shoot him,"

a Black middle-aged woman attempts to intervene.

"Stand back," the other cop
shouts to her and the growing crowd
who are ridiculing the officer and videoing the stop.

It's happening to me.
I panic. I just want to be free.
The fear of getting in the back of that squad car.
I can't breathe.
He grabs my bound
hands and attempts to pull me to my feet.
"Stop resisting," he says, burying my face in the pavement.
"Get off me," I shout.
The crowd keeps growing and drawing closer.
The other officer calls for backup.
Now there are five cops on the scene.
Their response is extreme.

I don't have a weapon.
I just want to breathe.
"Get off him," Jay D says.
"Stand back, Jay D," I say.
I writhe on the ground as if I'm having an epileptic fit.
I feel a kick.
Followed by another and then another.
Someone from the crowd shouts, "Stop kicking the little brother."
His words catch Officer Hyatt's attention.
"Yeah, we got you live," a teenage girl shouts,
"and we gonna make sure this video goes viral."
The situation had spiraled
into an all too familiar case of a Black man

being the victim of police brutality.
He's determined to arrest a Black for inciting the school riot,
and harassing me is just a formality.

Officer Hyatt motions for his comrades to stand down.
He removes the handcuffs
and hands me back my keys.
"I'm gonna let you go this time, but if you so much as sneeze,
I'm taking you down."
"Are you alright, man?" Jay D asks.
I nod, too exhausted to talk.
I am really feeling the stress.
I take a moment to decompress,
to process what just happened to me,
and the reason for the disconnect
between cops and Blacks.
How can you build trust and feel safe
when those committing the crimes
against you are the very ones sworn to serve and protect your life?
As the crowd disperses, I get message alerts
like "Bruh, you alright? I just seen you online."
"That was so messed up what 12 did to you."
"Man, those cops crossed the line."
Hitman heard about what happened.
He gives me a ride home.

"What they did to you was pretty jacked up," he says.
"They'll do anything to keep us from getting the message out,
that what was done and is still being done to us ain't right."
"That cop picked a fight.

He wanted a reason to put a bullet in my head.
Hitman, do you think all White cops are racist?"
"Nah," Hitman replies, "but I think it's like they said
during the LA riots,
'Police are trained to approach Black men
as criminals first and citizens second.'"
"You believe they are trained that way."
"Maybe not at the academy," Hitman replies,
"but yeah, they've been programmed like that.
Unfortunately for us, that is how they see us, lil bro."

I thank Hitman for the ride home
and for the talk on the way.
Jay D gets off at my house.
The news of the cops pummeling me arrived home before
I did.
Mama is waiting at the door.
She cradles me in her arms as I sob.
Every inch of my body throbs
with pain.
"You don't have nothing to be ashamed of," she says, lifting
my chin.
"I tried to do like you taught me, but then this officer starts trippin'
and—"
"And you kept your wits about you," Mama consoles.
"In a situation like that, it is easy to lose control,
but you made it back home.
A live dog is better than a dead lion,"
she says, running me a salt bath.

I am alive, but a part of me hasn't returned home.
A part of me is still on that gravel pavement
wrestling with a bad cop,
a cop who made a bold statement,
that the men and women in blue aren't afraid to use excessive force
even if the heat was on them for killing that Black pizza delivery driver.
It's called under color of the law.
I'd like to think of racism as a human flaw,
but it's so much more than that.
It's like a malignant growth that metastasizes
until it destroys all the healthy diversity cells.
It compels
people to despise a person because of skin color,
to hate people they don't even know.

I've faced racism before,
but when that officer threw me on the ground,
I felt so helpless, like racism had won,
until I heard people shouting, "Let him go."
That's when I realized the war wasn't done.
We can't let racism win.
We can't.
If it means marching and protesting,
whatever it takes to make our voices be heard.
Racism won't win.

I have to stay home from school a few days.
That is okay
because it gives me time to soak it all in.
I need a mental break.

Besides, there isn't a part on my body that doesn't ache.
I am the new hashtag.
People are online hashtagging "justice for Mason".
Some take it to the street
and demonstrate in front of the police station.
When I return to school,
everyone or almost everyone is glad
to see me.
I hear a few sighs of relief.
I'm certain I see a mist in Ms. Jordan's eyes
as she welcomes me back.
I sit and listen as Emma, Kabria, and DeAndre
share their creative writings with the class,
but the students appear more interested in what
happened to me than listening to others read or recite their poetry.
Ms. Jordan asks if there is something I want to share.
I reply that I have written about my experience,
entitled "Under Color of Law."

Under Color of Law

There's a scar, right here, I point at my head.
It's not visible because of my hair.
Just like you can't see that scar,

There are other scars you can't see,
like the ones that keep me up at night,
the ones that cause me to break out in a cold sweat.

The ones I wish I could forget.
No one ever thinks that it will happen to them.
I never thought it would happen to me,
that I would be a victim of police brutality.

But it happened.
It was real.
I've watched videos of police officers gunning down
unarmed Black men.

I've been stopped for looking suspicious,
with nothing in my hands.
I've been handcuffed and questioned
and coerced into making a confession
saying I committed a crime of which I had no part.
I've been punched and accused of resisting arrest
under color of authority.
I'm only free because of a technicality.
If it hadn't been for the people watching, going live on social media,

I may have been another fatality.
All my life, I've been taught to respect the law,
but who knew I had to watch my six
with cops in the mix?

Thousands of viewers shared the video

of me being beaten and kicked,
and they're told they didn't see
what they know they saw.
>A Black man.
>A blue uniform.
>A gun.
>A badge
and the law on the officer's side
and cops get away with homicide
>under Color of Law.

"What about all the things the protesters get away with,"
says Connor, "like burning and looting businesses
and destroying property?
They don't respect authority."
"Yeah," says Jackson. "The protesters in Ferguson burned police cars.
Minneapolis protesters burned down the police precinct headquarters."
Jackson's cosigning for Connor, so I jump in the ring.
"After they got tired of police firing rubber bullets at them,
and spraying them with tear gas.
Burning and looting acts are post wars
in retaliation for all the violence perpetrated against Blacks."
Connor says Black Lives Matter protesters are thugs.
"Thugs, really?" I reply. "Oh, so you want to go there.
Let's take it to January 6."
Connor says, "What else would you call someone
who destroys government property?"
"I can think of a few names," I say, "Proud Boys, QAnon,
Oath Keepers."
Caroline doesn't want to talk about January 6,

so she says if it wasn't for the boys in blue,

we would have a lawless society.

"Like we did on January 6," I say.

Sweat appearing on her brow, face flushed.

Could it be anxiety?

Lynesha asks, "What happens when the cops become the opps?"

Caroline defends the uniform, saying that most cops are good

and they're just doing their jobs trying to keep law and order.

When they give a command, you should follow them.

If you don't, and you get shot, it's your fault.

DeAndre asks Caroline if she thinks it was Philando Castile's

fault that he got shot when he was following police orders.

Castile complied when the officer told him to get his ID

and still he ended up in the mortuary.

"The officer thought he was reaching for a gun," says Caroline.

I ask Caroline if she believes in Second Amendment rights.

She says she believes in the right to bear arms.

Then I tell her that Philando Castile had a right to bear arms.

He identified that he had a gun in the car for which he had a permit,

so why was he shot when he followed police orders?

The officer shot him in front of his four-year-old child.

A man like that is unfit

to wear the badge.

The last memory Philando Castile's daughter has of her father alive

was watching him die.

Taking Off the Blinders

If you can't sympathize, maybe you can empathize.
Imagine it's a beautiful summer evening,
and you are out riding.
   Your four-year-old daughter and her mother are passengers in your car.
You look in your rearview mirror.
You see what every driver dreads, blue lights.
The officer pulls you over because
you look like a robbery suspect,
but then again, all Black people look alike, right?
The officer says, "Hello, sir." You return the greeting.
As a Black man, you have been stopped so many times by police
that you know the drill.
You inform the officer that you have a firearm
on you for which you are licensed to carry.
You reach for your driver's license and registration,
although you may be wary,
   and he unloads seven rounds in you in front of your four-year-old.
You tell him as you are bleeding that you were reaching for your I.D.
Instead of administering first aid, he watches as you bleed out.
Although you are no longer a threat, he stands with his weapon drawn.
He does not attempt to save you. Does he care if you live or die?
He stands and waits for the paramedics to arrive.
He later says he shot you — not one time — but seven times
because he thought you were going for your gun.
But you have to wonder as you are dying
if he would have been so quick to draw his gun on a White motorist,
if he would have fired seven bullets into the body of a White man
with his child watching.

Your daughter tells her hysterical mother to calm down
because she doesn't want her shot by the police too.
"I don't want it to be like this anymore.
I wish this town was safer," the girl tells her mother.

Safer for who, you wonder, but you already know the answer.

At age four, your daughter has already learned

what it means to be Black in America.

Philando Castile is dead at age thirty-two.

The officer who shot and killed him blamed Philando for his actions

when the truth is Officer Jeronimo Yanez responded the way

he has been programmed to.

In this country, we have developed a tolerance for racial injustices.

But it is time that we say it's not okay.

The thing that has been happening to African Americans

and other people of color must stop today.

Each of us must become personally responsible for

our attitudes and actions toward gross injustices

against people of color.

It is time to take the blinders off and stop pretending

that racism is not real and that what is happening in our country

to people of color is not that bad. It is that bad.

Anyone who is not willing to admit that is a part of the problem.

Giving Mama Her Due

The next day at class, Ms. Jordan greets us in her usual way.
She never has much to say
about the topics we discuss.
The poetry class often feels more like
a social studies debate than a poetry class.
History and current events are topics of conversation
spoken through verse.
This wasn't what I expected when I signed up for this course,
but I don't have any remorse.
If anything it helps me understand why Mama fights so hard
to keep me out the streets.
She isn't a single parent, but my dad drives trucks
and is away from home most of the time.
My mama took upon her the uphill climb
of raising teen boys.
Although my brother is now in his first year of college,
I have to give Mama her props.
I owe a big thanks to Ms. Franklin too.
Everyone should have a school counselor
who pushes you to go beyond your limits.
I thought I knew all there was about
writing lyrics and creating beats,
but this poetry class has made me reach.

Today Hadley presents first. Her poem is brief,
but she shares her truth
as proof
that racism is alive and thriving.

White Privilege

Left the sports bar.
Crashed a brand-new car.
Wrong place. Wrong time.
I'm not worried.
Luckily for me, justice is blind.
Rich daddy called in a favor.
The judge is our neighbor.
It's called White privilege.

Racial Sympathy

"That's not White privilege.
That's a neighbor doing a neighbor a favor," says Jasmine.
Hadley still wants to prove that she is
sympathetic to our plight.
She says that when it comes to race, she's color-blind,
and that she
           DEFENDS BLACKS AGAINST RACISM ONLINE.
She says that she has supported BLM
much to the disappointment of her parents
and enrolled in the Black poetry class
despite how they feel about Blacks.
           All those facts should be proof enough that she is PRO-BLACK.
Fajah tells her that she is trying too hard to relate to us,
and it's coming across as pity
and that we don't want pity.
We want to be treated fairly,
not as a project or sympathetic object
           but recognized as people, as individuals, AS EQUALS.

Jamir volunteers to go next.
His poem is called "Driving While Black."

Driving While Black

He approaches my car.

    Do I reach for my driver's license and registration?

      Will he accuse me of reaching for a pole?

        I place both hands on my dash to prove that I'm not a threat.

          But he's not satisfied.

            He wants a confrontation.

              He barks commands like show me your hands.

                When I say what do you mean?

                  He calls for backup.

                  Now there are four officers on the scene.

                  When you're Black,

                  there's nothing routine about

                  a traffic stop.

                  The first officer pulls me from my car

                and throws me on the ground.

              Where are the drugs? he asks.

            When I tell him there are none,

           he points a gun at my head.

          I close my eyes 'cause I know I'm dead.

        He pounds my face in the pavement

        and shouts racial slurs.

      His brothers in blue join in,

      beating and kicking me,

    emasculating me as a Black man.

    Handcuffs on my wrists.

  Never learned to control my fists.

But while they're bound behind my back

cops say I tried to resist.

Their word against mine.

Looks like I'm gonna do some time.

Graduated from the school of fist,

 No more hand-to-hand combat.

  Niggas carrying guns.

   Went to Catholic school

    Ran by a bunch of nuns

     Taught me to turn the other cheek

     But that's for the weak.

     Easy to say when you never lived on my street.

     The hood is a jungle.

     You're either the predator or the prey.

    Either way, life ain't no beach.

   Nah it's a dog eat dog world.

  It ain't no oyster.

 I ain't looking for a pearl,

just respect.

But those who are sworn to serve and protect

only see my ebony skin.

God only knows

the trouble it gets me in.

An education, a good reputation means nothing.

 I'm profiled wherever I go.

  If I call the suburbs my home,

   neighbors call the police,

    a way of telling me I don't belong.

     Cops take one look at me, my skin that is,

      and that's all they see before determining I'm guilty

       of whatever crime they want to pin on me.

     Whether I'm walking, riding, or sleeping in my bed,

it's all the same. No one cares to know my name.
Whether I'm the Black guy in sweats and a hoodie
or an Armani suit,
I'm the Black guy.

———

Ladarius has something to say about surviving the jungle of racism.

Survival of the Fittest

Survival of the fittest.
The strong overpowering the weak,
it doesn't seem fair
when you're the one feeling the heat,
but what can you do
when the rules have already been set?
Do you just give it your best shot
and take what you can get?

Survival of the fittest
The strong overpowering the weak,
drowning in your tears,
and tired of losing sleep.
What can you do when you aren't allowed to choose,
and it's already been predetermined
who will win or lose?
When the odds are against you
and you try to win but stumble and fall
and you jump over hurdles
but hit a brick wall.

Survival of the fittest
The strong overpowering the weak,
the gazelle has to escape
and the lion has to eat.

Survival of the fittest.
Endurance at its best.
In the end,
predator and prey both need to rest.

Nonconformance

Jamarcus comments that White people are oppressors by nature.
Connor replies, "If we are oppressive by nature,
does that make you weak by nature?"
Ladarius says our people are weak as a result of oppression.
Caroline says that Black people's failure to thrive
is not the White man's transgression
and she wonders if we ever get tired of playing the victim.
"Shut up, Karen," says Fajah.
Caroline replies with a malign expression
that her name is not Karen.
"Oh, you are a Karen alright."
Fajah flails her hands in the air.
"'Call the police. A Black man's looking at me.
I feel threatened.'"

"You don't need the police. You need an Oscar for your performance."
Caroline looks at Fajah. "You're mad because you can't be me."
"You don't have anything I want," says Fajah.
"You're mad because of my nonconformance."
"Like conforming to using a hairbrush," says Caroline.

"What did you say?" Fajah tilts her head to the side.
"Becky with the good hairs sayin' yo head shaggy," says DeAndre.

"My hair is natural. I don't need you
with your bleached blonde shadow roots hair
telling me to what to do with mine."
Fajah pats her 4C curly locks.

"I like my hair the way it is,
so excuse me if I don't fit into your White box."

"Speaking of White box, isn't that what Jasmine is trying to do with
the platinum blonde wig?" says Caroline.

Jasmine looks back.
She heard Caroline call her name, but she doesn't have all the facts.
"She saying you wearing a wig 'cause you bald-headed," says DeAndre.
"I know she just didn't put my name in her mouth," says Jasmine.
"I'm about to have a three-day holiday."

Jasmine takes off her hoop earrings
that are large enough to wear on her wrists.
"Jazz, we ain't about that life," I say.
"Use your head, not your fists."

"She don't know the first thing 'bout Black girl hair," says Jasmine.
"Then school her," I say.
Jasmine turns to Caroline.
"This," Jasmine points to her blonde wig, "is a protective hairstyle.
I wear it to keep from damaging my real hair."
Jasmine pulls off her wig.
"That is so ghetto," says Caroline.
Jasmine peels off her wig cap,
revealing her thick cornrows.
"This is how my hair grows
healthy and strong.
Whatever you think about Black girls wanting
to be White, you got it all wrong.

We don't want your ivory world.

We just like variety."

The Black girls cheer Jasmine on while the White girls stare.

Caroline tosses her hair over her shoulder.

"That is so White girl." Jaquesha tosses her braided extensions over her shoulder.

"So now you all want to gang up on me." Caroline shakes her head.

"Typical Black people."

"Typical Karen," says Fajah.

Caroline looks like she is about to explode but maintains her composure.

"Ms. Jordan, I'm ready to share my poem. It is called "The Victim.""

The Victim

What's it like to be a victim of the system?
Just ask anyone who's Black or Brown.
They can tell you all about how the White man
works so hard to keep them down.
Denying them opportunities,
forcing them to commit crimes,
pressuring them to make poor decisions
because they need bodies to fill prisons.
Victims of systemic oppression.
Systems that provide them with low-income housing,
SNAP benefits to keep food on the table,
welfare checks to people who are capable
of holding jobs,
but they'd rather not get paid,
then they'd have to give up their Medicaid.
But then again, the system is against people of color.
It's such a shame they were born with Black or Brown skin.
I guess all these benefits of systemic oppression
are nails in their coffin.

———

"All those free benefits don't add up to over
two hundred years of free labor," says Fajah.
With her gaze bouncing between Hunter and Fajah, Emma says,
"I don't think it's fair to refer to Blacks as victims in a sarcastic way,
but what I don't understand is why are you always so angry?"
Khalan gives her the stare down. "You just heard about our dilemma,
and you still have questions, so I'll tell you why.

I'm angry, a truth I cannot deny,
for I live with the residual effects of days gone by,
days when injustice still rears its ugly head,
days that tell me that the Jim Crow laws were right
and for my freedom, I must fight,
days that remind me of the shedding
of my people's blood.
When crimes against me go unpunished
simply because of the color of my skin,
and in spite of how hard I try,
I just can't seem to win.
Yeah, that makes me angry."

Emma says she still doesn't think she would be that angry if she were Black.
Lynesha says that's because Emma's parents never had to have the talk.
"The talk? What's the talk?" Emma asks.
"Oh, so you don't know about the talk," says Lynesha.
Emma asks Lynesha if by the talk, she means sex and drugs.
"For you, that would be the all-Black-men-are-thugs talk," says Ladarius.
"My parents are deceased, and when they were living, I never heard
them use those words."
Lynesha doesn't have a comeback.
She is drowning, so I gotta help a sister out.

The Talk

Depending on who you are,
THE TALK can mean different things to people of different cultures.
While most parents talk to their kids about sex, drugs, or stranger danger,
Black families talk to their kids about what it means to be
BLACK IN AMERICA.
THE TALK comes with warnings about vultures
who prey on people of Black and Brown cultures, who view us as weak,
abusing their authority and expecting us to be meek.
The first things your parents tell you when they sit you down
to have THE TALK is that you will not always be treated fairly,
even when you dot the i's and cross the t's.
At some point, every Black family will have "THE TALK"
with their children to prepare them for moments like,
"He stopped me for nothing,
and I wasn't even doing anything wrong."
Black kids are taught responses like
always keep YOUR HANDS VISIBLE.
If the officer yells at you,
reply in a nonthreatening tone.
We are told that we need to WORK TWICE AS HARD as our
White peers
if we want to get ahead,
and to pay more attention to the facts than what is said.
We are told that we WILL BE DENIED well-deserved promotions,
and like George Floyd, we will feel that knee in our neck
that insists on removing our respect
and yet we must FIGHT TO RISE ABOVE it all
when progress seems to stall.

Even when we are blamed for things that are clearly not our fault,
we must REMEMBER "THE TALK."

Ms. Jordan asks how many Black students in class
have had "the talk" with their parents.
Fourteen students raise their hands in the air, including Kabria and Javier.
Lynesha says that her parents had "The Talk" with her
and her grandparents had the talk with them,
and that it would be nice if she didn't have to have the talk with her kids.
Hunter says his parents had "The Talk" with him and warned
of people who want to cancel culture.
"Oh yeah," says Tayvion. "My parents warned me to beware of vultures,
birds of prey who tear the flesh from the bone
to make themselves strong.
We have to fight for equal rights.
Our demands for justice only get noticed when there's mayhem.
Like Breonna's Law, banning no-knock search warrants,
changes made postmortem."
Hunter brings up affirmative action and says that because
of affirmative action Blacks have better jobs
and get accepted into Ivy League universities.

Boiling Point

Ladarius scoffs, leaning back in his chair.
"Do you have something you want to share?"
Ms. Jordan asks.
"Yeah," Ladarius replies.
"I'm tired of the lies.
America made promises she didn't keep,
and now she expects us to rise while we'd rather just weep
over four hundred years of oppression
when we started out with nothing.
We took nothing and built with that,
and now you want to take our nothing back
because we exceeded your expectations.
We waited on reparations
that never came.
Our successes you claimed
and our failures you blamed
on us wasting opportunities,
opportunities we never got."

"You got plenty of opportunities," Connor interrupts,
breaking Ms. Jordan's rules.
"You got opportunities that should have gone
to someone more qualified,
but because you were Black,
you were moved to the front of the line."

"It's about time,"
says Jaquesha.

"We get tired of looking at the back of your head."

"Are you two done?" Ladarius asks.
Jaquesha rolls her eyes.
"No, but say what you got to say
'cause I got something to say too."

"Okay," Ladarius replies,
"But don't interrupt me until I'm through."

Jaquesha nods,
but Connor looks the other way.
He doesn't want to hear
anything Ladarius has to say.

Martin's Dream

If this country was true to its word,
there would be no need for affirmative action.
Martin Luther King, Jr. said it best.
"All we say to America is, 'Be true to what you said on paper.'"
It would be nice if people always played by the rules
and lived by Dr. King's dream
that we could live in a nation where we wouldn't be judged
by the color of our skin, but by the content of our character.
That is still a dream and not a present reality,
and until the dream becomes a reality,
affirmative action is needed to level the playing field.
Equal rights begin with equal opportunities.
Where equal opportunities do not exist,
the need for affirmative action does."
"If you ask me, it's reverse racism," says Caroline.
"According to the Cambridge dictionary,
a level field is a situation in which everyone
has the same chance of succeeding,"
Jaquesha says, reading from her iPad.

I can't believe my ears.
Jaquesha knows the purpose of a dictionary
and how to use one.
As if she knows what I am thinking,
and not me only, but probably every student in class,
"I do read more than fashion magazines," she says.
"Maybe not that old boring stuff
that was written centuries ago, but I do read.

Since being in this class,
I've been thinking about more than just fashion.
I have something to say about affirmative action.
Anyone who claims that policies
intended to create equal opportunities
for people who have experienced such atrocities
            as being handed down a LEGACY OF SLAVERY,
voter suppression, Black codes and Jim Crow laws
and having to start over with little more
than the clothes on your back
and laws created to oppress you,
to keep you from rising to the top,
            people who are saying these things, need to
            STOP LYING TO THEMSELVES
and give us our props.
We have taken your discarded entrails and made soul food.
We have worked as sharecroppers and produced crops
only to be told that we could not enjoy the profits of our labor,
and you feel as if you are doing us a favor.
            Affirmative action was earned
            WHEN THE FIRST SLAVE SHIPS CAME."

"I'm not in favor of affirmative action," says Emma.
"I'm in this chair, but I don't expect special privileges
because I can't walk."
"Yeah, you do," says Fajah. "You want things handicap accessible,
like wider doors and wheelchair ramps."
"That's different," says Emma. "I didn't ask to be in this chair."
"But you need accessibility to be able to do
what people with mobility do," says Fajah.

"What if I said special accommodations for wheelchairs aren't fair?"

"You're comparing apples to oranges," says Caroline.

"You can't move forward living in the past.
You can't hold people in the present responsible
for what people did in the past.
I agree with Emma, I just don't think affirmative action is fair.
It's like people are being punished now
for what somebody, who they never met, did hundreds of years ago.
Why should I not be able to get a job that I'm qualified for
because my ancestors owned slaves?"

"Y'all got what you wanted," says Khalan.

"Affirmative action can no longer be used in college admissions,
so rich people can go back to making phone calls and contributions
to get their kids into their dream college."

"My parents are working middle class." Caroline defends
her position. "I don't expect them to make any phone calls,
because I made the grades to get into college.
I, personally, will be happy when affirmative action ends."

"You know what I think," says Jaquesha.

"I think we would be happy if there was no reason
for us to need affirmative action."

Affirmative Action

Level the playing field,
and there will be no need for me.
Do away with partiality, and my face you will never see.
Give people of color a chance just like their fellow man,
and I will gladly seek a retirement plan.
Judge each candidate by his qualifications
and not the color of his skin,
and I will fade away like a feather in the wind.
Treat all men fairly, giving each what's right,
and I will disappear like a shadow into the night.
Take away the glass ceiling,
and obstacles that bar the door,
and I will bid you farewell.
You will hear from me no more.

———

After Jaquesha presents a debatable argument
about affirmative action, Hunter and Khalan get into it
over saluting the flag.
Hunter says refusing to salute dishonors our nation
and that every US citizen should be made to salute the flag.
Khalan says this country's founders
did not write the Constitution with people of color in mind.
Khalan contends that Hunter is proud of a history he does not know.
Khalan says he's ready to present.
Class ends. The presentation will have to wait until tomorrow.

The next day, Khalan is sitting with a history book

in poetry class. He doesn't look
up when Jasmine walks by wearing a skirt
that breaks school dress code.
Ms. Jordan calls roll, and before she has a chance
to ask who's ready to present,
Khalan is standing in front of her desk
holding an American flag.
Hunter looks as if he's about to explode.

A Nation's Hypocrisy

When the framers wrote the Constitution,
they did not have enslaved Africans in mind.
While some argue that freeing enslaved Africans
during the colonies' freedom from British control
was ill-timed,
I say that was the poorest excuse of its kind.
How could the colonists not think that it was right
to free slaves when colonists were willing to fight
for their own freedom?

Standing Against Hypocrisy!

That is what Frederick Douglass did
when he stood before a crowd of White Americans
as they were celebrating their country's freedom,
and he gave his "What to the Slave is the Fourth of July?"
speech on July 5, 1852,
but you don't hear about that in the history books, do you?

———

Khalan pauses and looks around at his audience before continuing.

Sitting Against Hypocrisy

On December 1, 1955, when Rosa Parks refused
to give up her seat to a White man,
she challenged this nation's segregated seating policy.

——

Khalan sounds like a fire-baptized preacher rearing back on his heels
and digging deeper for words that will stir the hearts and minds of his
audience, and when he finds them, he preaches like it's his last sermon,
for it could very well be for all he knows.

Taking a Knee Against Hypocrisy

When Colin Kaepernick took a knee on Sep. 1, 2016,
as the national anthem was being sung,
he was doing the same thing, challenging a nation's hypocrisy.
Sometimes you have to be willing to stand, sit, and even kneel
for what you believe in.

———

Caroline says she believes the framers were good people,
and that Khalan is making them out to be bad.
Fajah does the neck roll. She's about to set the record straight.
"Imagine being counted by your government as three-fifths of a person.
Would you hold those lawmakers in high regard?
Would you force your children to accept that men
who wrote about civil liberties for White citizens
while denying freedom to enlaved Blacks were their heroes?"

"Those were just the times they lived in.
Slavery was a part of American life back then," says Emma.

"They went to Africa and kidnapped Africans.
They kidnapped people and forced them into slave labor.
There was nothing good or right about that," says Fajah.

"She's trying to explain to you that those were the times they were
living in," says Hunter.
"I get what she's saying. I just don't agree with her," says Fajah.
"That's because you want to erase history," says Hunter.
"And you want to rewrite it," says Fajah.

Hunter bares his teeth like a snarling dog.

"You're trying to cancel culture."

"And you want to make America great again.

You and your demagogue.

For the record, we are not attempting to cancel culture.

'Whether a tree falls toward the north or the south,

the place where the tree falls is where it stays.'"

Hunter gets out of his seat and goes and stands beneath
the wall-mounted American flag.

MAGA

Hunter's lips curve slightly
in a screw-you smile.
"Yes," he says, "I believe in making America great again.
Just look at the state this country is in.
Terrorists living among us,
and we don't even know who they are
or what they are planning
because we are so afraid of banning
entrance into our country.

"No, instead, we make it all comfy —
public housing, food stamps, Medicaid.
Of course, they came and stayed.
Let's make America a country where people like my dad
don't have to worry about losing their jobs to illegals,
or American jobs moving overseas,
or paying higher taxes,
their wallets feeling the squeeze
while welfare queens sit at home on their thrones.

"And now you want to take away our rights to bear arms,
a man's rights to keep his wife and children safe from harm.
You criticize us because we are in favor of building a wall.
If we are going to make this country great again,
we have to stop making it a free-for-all."

——

Jasmine, who is wearing her hair back
for the first time since poetry class started,
turns to Hunter and asks, "When?"
"When what?" he says.
"When was America great?" she asks.

When?

You say you want to make this country great again.
That implies that it was great before,
but everything you're saying sounds like folklore.
I just want to know when.
When was this country so great?
It is time to set the record straight.
Was it during slavery or the Reconstruction period?
Was it the Trail of Tears?
I heard replicas of the Cherokee Rose make nice souvenirs.
Was it the Jim Crow or Post-Civil Rights Movement era
when the Ku Klux Klan terrorized people of color
and would set a man on fire in front of his child and its mother?
Was it the LA Riots when Black communities protested police brutality,
or was it the reality
of seeing children in cages
or undocumented immigrants being cheated of fair wages?
I would like to know when America was in her finest hour.
Show me your points of praise,
so I can rejoice with you about dem good ole days.

———

"I think we need to stop focusing on color," says Emma.
"Personally, I don't like the saying 'Black lives matter'. All lives matter."
"What you just said is hurtful, dismissive, and borderline cruel.
You can't just dismiss our pain.
We never discounted the value of all human life.
We just want the world to know that our lives matter
as much as other lives," says Jasmine.

Emma folds her arms across her chest,
which means she isn't bending on her stance.
Jamir closes his eyes and tilts his head back,
then stands to his feet as if to say, *"Let's do this."*

All Lives Matter

Wrongful killings.
Gruesome and chilling.
Saying all lives matter is like fresh wounds added to old scars.
Would you prefer that I was dead or behind bars?
If you believe all lives matter, then why are Black bodies
the ones lying in the street
pleading to breathe?

——

Ms. Jordan's face turns blood red.
I can only imagine the thoughts
going through her head.
No diss,
but I don't believe Ms. Jordan signed up for this.
But I got to give her props
for hanging in there.
Most teachers I know would have quit after the first week.
This class may not be what any of us expected,
but it is giving tea
when it comes to discussing issues that affect the Black community.
I just hope Ms. Jordan doesn't expect unity
because I ain't never gonna see eye to eye with Connor or Caroline.
They got their views, and I got mine.

At the end of class, Ms. Jordan announces that we will be writing
our thoughts on Critical Race Theory for homework.
Caroline is quick to point out that this is not an American
Government class

and that CRT is not on the syllabus. News flash. The syllabus states that assignments are subject to change at the instructor's discretion.

Responsibilities and Consequences

Caroline lowers her gaze.
"I have straight A's, and now because of this class,
I'm in danger of dropping my grades."
Ms. Jordan smiles placidly.
"Just do your assignments as instructed, and you'll be fine."
Caroline exhales sharply.
"You said in the syllabus that classroom participation
is 30% of our grade.
I can't pretend that I'm okay
talking about racism.
I'm made to feel like a racist when I speak up,
and when I keep silent, I feel like a hypocrite.
I just don't fit
in this class,
and I don't want to just pass.
I want to maintain my GPA.
Next year I'll be a senior,
and I want to graduate top of my class."
Again, Ms. Jordan smiles a tight-lipped smile.
"Caroline, you have a right to your opinion,
but you need to understand that other students
have a right to theirs."
Caroline rolls her eyes.
"You're not the one who has to deal
with all the angry looks and stares."
"Caroline, you signed up for this class
of your own free will,"
Ms. Jordan gently scolds. "No one forced you to take it.

You knew it was a Black poetry class
and still
you signed up for it."
"I didn't know that this was going to be a
slam poetry class."
"It's creative writing relating to the Black experience.
What were you expecting to write about?"
Ms. Jordan's brow furrows.
"Not about how evil White people are,"
Caroline replies. "You can't expect me to write about being
Black when I don't know what it feels like to be Black,
and right now, I feel like I'm under attack
from you and my classmates of color."

Ms. Jordan's smile slips.
"On the first day of class, I said you have the power of choice,
and that power comes with responsibilities
and consequences."
Caroline twists her mouth in a soured expression.
"I know Ms. Franklin is not going to allow me to change classes,
which means I'm stuck
in this class, and that really sucks,
so, I guess I got to listen to what they have to say,
and they have to listen to what I have to say."

Different Points of View

"I am not asking anyone to agree with the
opinions of others, only to respect their points of view,"
Ms. Jordan responds.
Caroline nods.
I applaud Ms. Jordan's efforts.
There is no denying, I have to give her credit for trying
to create a civilized dialogue between Blacks and Whites.
But now she has unleashed the beast.
The Critical Race Theory could bring out
the best or worst in anybody.
Critical Race Theory is one of those topics
that has a way of making people feel uncomfortable —
Blacks feel as if the system has placed them at a disadvantage
and yet requires them to work harder and perform better than White
Americans,
only to be denied the same rights and privileges as Whites.
Whites feel as if they've built a democratic society
where people of all races are provided opportunities,
and the American dream
is like a ticket that only has to be redeemed
to enjoy privileges as American citizens.
They say why should they be blamed
for things that occurred
long before they were born.
Different points of view
for a conversation that is long overdue.

At home, I ask a weary Mom her thoughts

on the Critical Race Theory.
She works all day, but still manages to make
time for me as she always did
ever since I was a thumb-sucking little kid.
Mama, what do you think about the Critical Race Theory being
taught in schools?
Does your high school teach American history?
Of course, it does.
Didn't you take social studies classes in elementary and middle school?
Yes, ma'am.
Did they teach about slavery and the Indian Removal Act?
We were taught that slaves were brought to America
to work on rice plantations and help
with the harvesting of cotton and sugarcane.
We were told that some slave masters were cruel,
but most of them were good people who treated their slaves well.
We also learned about indentured servants.
What did they teach you about the Indians and the settlers?
We learned about how an Indian named Squanto
helped the settlers to grow their crops
and that because of conflicts between the settlers,
the Indians were removed from their homeland.
What else did they teach you?
We memorized the preamble to the Constitution
and learned about famous war heroes
that fought during the Revolutionary War
and the War between the States.
We learned about the Ku Klux Klan and civil rights leaders.
Things like that.
Oh.

Mama, you never answered my question.

I believe history should be taught as accurately as possible.
That includes the good and the bad.
I don't believe in sugarcoating it to spare anyone's feelings
or to keep from showing anyone in a bad light.
What was done is done.
You can't do nothing to change it,
but we can all learn from it and grow from it.
Now what would be more unjust than what happened to people of color
is to pretend that it never happened,
and that's what banning the Critical Race Theory is asking us to do —
pretend that these things that have helped to shape who we are
as Black Americans never happened.
As my grandmother would say, "That's adding insult to injury,"
and you can't expect a person to just be okay with that.

Some Whites feel as if we're blaming them for the past.

It's not about blaming this generation for sins of the past,
but they have a right to know the truth.
This country has an ugly history.
It makes me sad to think about all of them slaves
brought here against their will.
All the hangings and killings.
So much blood was shed, but it's still a part of history.
It doesn't do any good to pretend it never happened.
That won't change the fact that it did.
It doesn't do any good to be angry about the past.
It's what we deal with now that angers me.
It's like we haven't learned anything from the past.
I hate to see young Black men throwing away their futures,
spending twenty and thirty years in prison

when the slaves risked their lives to be free,
a war was fought for their freedom.
That's why I want you to stay out of trouble, Mason.
You're smart. You have a lot to offer this world.
You won't do yourself or anyone else any good behind bars.
Mama, why did you get involved in the BLM movement?
I did it for you.
My heart dropped every time I heard
about fatal police shootings of Black men.
My heart bled for their mothers,
and I thought about how any one of those young men killed
could have been my son,
and when those cops beat you, it almost was my son.

Penning My Thoughts

After talking to Mama, I go to my room
and surf the net
to collect
information
on what made
the CRT such a threat
and why it upsets
so many people.
I listen to speeches
by civil rights leaders,
and read about famous abolitionists,
and racists.
I read excerpts of documents
upon which this country
was founded
and the laws that compounded
the problem of race relations.
I begin to write.
I stay up half the night
penning my thoughts,
preparing to express
or defend
my beliefs
regarding the Critical Race Theory
grounded in truth
based upon this country's history.

A soft thud, a pause, then another more forceful thud

against my bedroom door interrupts my flow. It is Mama.

"Come in," I say.

"Mason." She smiles a close-lipped smile before continuing.

"I never told you this, but I used to write poetry back in the day."

"Why did you stop?"

"I don't know. I guess I got so busy,

but I thought about what's been going on in our country

and even closer to home.

All of this violence didn't start weeks ago or a year ago or five years ago.

It goes back farther than that. I've been so worried about your safety that

I have been guilty of holding you back.

You have a gift. With that gift you also have a responsibility.

We've got enough loose cannons around here going off on violent tantrums.

You understand what I'm saying." She nods.

"Yes, ma'am. I understand," I reply, then add,

"Mama, if you ever decide to pick up a pen again,

I'd like to hear some of your poetry."

Mama smiles. "Maybe someday." She nods

before closing the door behind her,

leaving me once again to my thoughts.

Banning the Truth

The next day at school, Ms. Jordan greets us with a grimace.
I know something is wrong before she hits us with the news
that we are about to lose
the one thing that allows us to speak our truth —
THE BLACK POETRY CLASS.
Hadley's parents were on a mission to deprogram her
after they discovered that she was dating a Black guy.
Dude doesn't even go to Dickerson.
He attends Camden High.
Somehow they got it in their heads
that Hadley met him through the poetry class.
They want the class removed from the curriculum,
or at minimum, canceled for the rest of the year.
They blame the class for fostering left-wing beliefs.
The school board blamed the poetry class for the school riot.
None of us were involved,
so why should we keep quiet
and allow people who had never been in our class
to decide our fate?
Maybe we could persuade them to change their minds.

At any rate,
we are not going to stand by and allow that to happen,
not without a fight.
Mama always says I am headstrong.
She is right.
"NAH!" I shout, standing to my feet.
"I need this class to graduate."

"So do I," says Caroline.

We are all feeling the heat.

"I guess I'll see you at the board meeting," I reply.

My classmates and I have our differences,

but for once we are unified.

We are determined to save the Black poetry class

from those who want to ban

how we express our views on historical and current events.

While some believe in our cause, others are on the fence.

"The school board meets next Tuesday," says Ms. Jordan.

"The meeting is open to the public to talk further about this subject.

Parents that are opposed to this class will be at the board meeting.

I think it is important that the board hears from you."

We know what we have to do.

When I tell Mama about the school board's plans

to cancel the Black poetry class,

Mama nods and picks up her cell phone fast.

She calls in reinforcements.

We are not against the school board alone

in our quest.

On Tuesday, one by one we stand up at the board meeting and express

why the poetry class should remain a part of the school curriculum,

but the board is not impressed.

We are regarded as just a bunch of kids

who don't know what is best,

so it is up to our parents to persuade the board,

but there are parents present that ignore

everything we say.

"Our children are being influenced by cancel culture,
and we must put a stop to it now," says Tyler Moore's dad.
"We cannot allow
our children's minds to be poisoned
with dangerous content.
I believe my concerns represent
the majority of parents here,
and those that couldn't be in attendance tonight."
"You don't represent me," says Fajah's mom,
"and you don't respect the arts.
Langston Hughes and other great poets wrote about racism.
What you want is escapism,
but you can't escape from the truth and neither can they.
Our children are faced with these issues every single day.
Now we are telling them they can't write about social justice issues.
Isn't that just another right that you are trying to refuse?
How can we ever expect social change if we silence them?
Why are you so afraid of a poem?"

"This is not about respecting the arts or Black poetry.
What Ms. Jordan is allowing to go on in her class is cancel culture,"
says another White parent.
"This kind of teaching swoops down like a vulture,
ripping from the minds of our children
every good thing this country stands for
by telling them that our founding fathers were horrible people."

"Freedom of speech is legal,"
says Jaquesha's mom.

Caroline's dad addresses the board next.
"I say we let the kids finish out this school year.
If we cancel the class now, the consequences could be severe.
I am concerned as anybody about cancel culture,
but Caroline needs this class to graduate,
a decision like this can wait
until next school term."
"Are you forgetting that this class caused a school riot?"
says Homer Hornbeck's mom.
Homer attended the poetry class the first two days
of the semester and never returned.

"Those are rumors that were never confirmed,"
says Caroline's dad.

"We don't have room for margin of error,"
Homer's mom continues.
"We must act now. Situations like this only get worse.
They don't get better."

"The poetry class isn't the problem.
It's what students are taught at home.
That's the problem," says Lynesha's mom.
"They are taught that history should be forgotten,
unless it makes heroes of people of fair skin."

"You people are always so hostile," says Jason Wahlberg's dad.

"Who are you calling you people," says Jamir's mom,
"and once again, you've proven my point.

Your problem started at home,
and now you're looking for someone to blame for the school riot
when it's people like you who created this hostile school climate."

"I think we've heard enough," says the board chair.
"We are ready to take a vote."
The school board votes 5-3 in favor of canceling the Black poetry class.
The ruling is just about to pass
when Mama steps forward.
The board chair objects,
but Mama shakes her head and opens her mouth
and tells a story that will leave no doubt
that we will not accept the school board's vote
to cancel the Black poetry class,
to cancel our history.

My History

I will not allow you to take away my history,
though it be filled with drudgery
of sugar plantations, tobacco and rice fields,
and cotton that yields
a white fluffy harvest compressed
into bales like my people who were oppressed
by slavers, overseers, and cruel taskmasters.
Failed attempts to run away from their captors
met with brute force. Freed men captured
and sold into slavery.
Though my dish be unsavory,
bitter as it may be,
it is MY HISTORY.
Though chapters of me have been deleted
from history books
and library shelves lie bare.
Though school boards vote to ban my truth,
and White parents are told beware,
though Critical Race Theory
is dismissed as nothing more than sophistry,
I will not allow you to take away MY HISTORY,
adding insult to injury.
I have a story that I must tell my children,
and they must tell their children.
Though it be filled with heartbreak and misery,
shackles, floggings, maimings, and hangings,
slave pits and slave markets,
people of dark skin used as cruel targets

of another's hatred.
Though it be an ugly truth, it is MY HISTORY.
Though it be filled with Black codes and Jim Crow laws,
struggle for freedom and unspeakable legislative flaws
that support discrimination against me.
Though my history be filled with White supremacy,
cross burnings, lynchings, and the heyday of the Ku Klux Klan.
It is MY HISTORY.
Though I be called words such as Negro,
n*gger, colored, spook, mongrel, and jigaboo,
mammy, pickaninny, spade, and boy.
Though it brings much joy
to those who wish to oppress me,
those who wish to hide the truth
because it reveals this nation's breech birth
and so it loses its esteemed worth
as a nation founded upon civil liberties and justice for all,
it is MY HISTORY.
Though your heroes are not my heroes
and your version of historical events
are told different from mine,
it will not change what happened —
not one single misdeed,
and though you have tried so diligently to conceal the truth,
you will not succeed,
because along with the pain and shame,
I have inherited a legacy
that refuses to be denied
as the blood of my people cries from the ground
saying tell my truth.

Tell it to every ear that will hear
and the ears that fear
the truth will change their perception
of this perfect history
that has been told of a nation that boasts of
freedom and liberty for all.
Tell it because it is so flawed.
A country with bloodstained hands that
refuses to wash them with truth,
omitting integral details
about the birth of this nation —
details of my labor, pain, and toil,
details of how I came to be on American soil.
Though you kidnapped me from my homeland,
stripped me of my culture,
forced me to learn your native tongue,
and took away my drums
that beat in harmony with the innermost part of me,
it is MY HISTORY.
Though I no longer wear chains around my ankles and wrists,
and I've learned to fight with words and not my fists,
justice still evades me.
Though I must prove that I deserve
the rights and privileges afforded Americans of fairer skin,
much to my chagrin,
it is MY HISTORY.
It is mine to embrace and not yours to erase.
Though it has blemishes and scars and has been marred,
I do not wish it away for it is who I am.
I am the shackled slave. I am the civil rights martyr.

I am the unarmed man on the ground begging to breathe,
and yet you want me to believe that my truth is not my truth.
For my forced servitude and humiliation,
I have been denied reparations,
and my history is filled with segregation,
voter suppression, hostile expressions
like "We don't serve coloreds here,"
the residue of being another man's possession.
Days like Bloody Sunday, the Watts and LA riots —
cruel acts of police brutality
still a present-day reality.
Whitewashed atrocities.
Denied opportunities.
Though my history be filled with much evil done to me,
it is MY HISTORY.
Though it be filled with loose and falling rocks
on this uphill climb,
it be mine,
ALL MINE.

————

The students from the poetry class clap and cheer.
Some parents cheer too.
The board chair taps his gavel.
The board's decision is starting to unravel
as one by one, the five opposing board members change their votes
in favor of keeping the Black poetry class, and now we finally have hope.

"Mama, that was tight!" I say. "You got mad skills.
Now I know where I got my skills.

Seriously, how could you keep that from me?"
Mama replies, "I told you that I wrote poetry back in the day."
"Well, you haven't lost your touch."
Jay D, Sultan, and Kaesan are impressed with Mom's skills too.
I wish Castille and Frederick were around to hear Mama do her thing,
but unfortunately, Castille and Frederick got kicked out of school
for their part in the school riot.
Why did they have to swing
on those boys.
Why couldn't they just walk away like I did.
They should have known it was being recorded.
I heard they both are facing possible jail time.
If they are lucky, they'll get probation.

What happened to them fueled my motivation
to use my head and not my fists.
I don't like being dissed,
but it's tough enough being a Black man.
It's even tougher for a Black man with a criminal record.
Frederick was destined to get locked up,
Castille ain't the jailbird type.
But when he took a swipe
at a White boy and it was caught on video,
I knew there was gonna be a clapback.
I ain't mad at him though.
Castille always gonna be my home boy.
Ain't nothing — not even jail — gonna destroy
our friendship.
That's real talk. Ain't no tongue slip.

I think about my bruhs, but I gotta keep going strong,
developing my craft.
The school board rescinds their decision
to cancel the class.
Still we are under the scrutiny of
disgruntled parents, teachers, and staff.

ACT 3

Room #104 Battle Rap

Ms. Jordan paces back and forth at the front of the class
as we enter.
We are ready for a CRT debate.
Uncensored.
No White parents, teachers, principals, or school board present
who feel the need to protect what we expected,
their White children from what they call harmful effects
of CRT.
We — the Black students — are free to reject
a picture-perfect version of historical events.
We can debate with our peers about CRT and cancel culture.
Ms. Jordan is treading uncharted waters,
but nothing ventured,
nothing gained.
However insane
her approach to teaching Black poetry,
we flowed in that vein.
After all, why should we complain?
They are our thoughts, our lyrics
about our triumph and our pain.
Ms. Jordan stops pacing.
We sit anxiously anticipating
what she has to say.
"I was warned by some of my coworkers
to leave the Critical Race Theory alone,
but it is a very relevant topic that hits close to home."
She sighs softly.
"CRT has a way of bringing out a lot of powerful emotions

and can make some people feel uncomfortable.
And although I'm all for self-expression,
I will not tolerate physical aggression
of any kind.
So, while you are sharing, please bear that in mind.
I would like to hear from all of you,
and that is almost impossible to do in one class
the way that we've been doing it;
therefore, we are going to do something a little different today.
What do you say
to a battle rap?"
I am the first to reply.
"Now that's what's up, Ms. Jordan," I shout.
"Let's do it," says Jamarcus.
We both are feeling this technique,
but not everyone shares our enthusiasm
for the spoken word.
Some people respond as if a battle rap
was a war cry.
Ms. Jordan says, "If you did your homework assignment, this activity
shouldn't be difficult at all. You can refer to your paper. Mason, I'm
going to ask you to start."
"Okay. I got this," I say.
Ms. Jordan smiles and nods. I can tell she's nervous about CRT,
especially after the riot, but maybe that's why there was a riot in the
first place, 'cause everybody dancing around the elephant in the
room, and the dance floor ain't but so big. Serious biz, I really respect
Ms. Jordan for doing this. Most teachers would run in the opposite
direction, but she ain't most teachers.

Critical Race Theory

Me

Critical Race Theory

White parents crying foul play

Attending school board meetings

To ban the truth.

Equal justice

As elusive as the fountain of youth.

Black heroes disappearing from American history —

Harriet Tubman, Rosa Parks,

And Martin Luther King remain a mystery,

Not to mention Black Wall Street,

Just another endeavor to keep us under your feet.

Blatant refusal to acknowledge the damage systemic racism has caused.

White privilege.

Institution and laws

Whose outcomes are determined by race, with lies they were laced

But you want us to remove the lens of racism

When talking about our country's history,

By denying the Critical Race Theory.

Africans, Indian Removal Act, Chinese immigrants

Theft of land and labor

Is how this country was built.

Cancel culture or is it White guilt?

Jamestown 1619

Human trafficking to the extreme

War between

The States

Lost

What a cost
To bring an end
To the legalized involuntary
Servitude of Black men, women, and children.
1865 slavery abolished,
But another form of slavery arose
Called Black codes.
Jim Crow
The Ku Klux Klan
For Whites only
School segregation
Brown versus the Board of Education
Ruby Bridges
The Little Rock Nine
Separate but equal.
Shame on this nation.

Hunter

If it wasn't for this nation and slavery
You'd be somewhere climbing a banana tree
Looking for food.

Zaquaisha

Hunter, I'm really not in the mood
To listen to you tell us why we should
Be grateful that the White man kidnapped
Our African ancestors and made them slaves
To save us from ourselves
When slavery was really about greed.
So, excuse me if I don't want to hear all about

What your people achieved
To make this nation great.

Emma

They weren't perfect. I'll give you that.
What makes you any better than them or us?
What you're doing is spreading a message of hate.
Regardless of their flaws, the Constitution,
The Bill of Rights were first rate.
So, give them the credit that they are due.
They paved a better way for me and you.

Ladarius

When the Constitution was written,
We were never a part of the equation
Until the North realized that the size of the population
Would affect their legislative representation,
So, they challenged the feasibility of equal representation.
But the Southern slaveholding states
Insisted on counting slaves
To increase their political voice,
Leaving the Northern states no other choice
But to reach a compromise on the size
Of the population counted for representation
And direct taxation.
Slaves would be counted
As three-fifths of a free person,
Which pleased the Southern slaveholding states
More representation
More political power to preserve the institution of slavery.

Those are the people you hail for their bravery.

Caroline

What they did or did not do about slavery
Has nothing to do with what's happening now.
Slavery was eradicated.
I think you're seeking to be validated
As a people.

Fajah

Slavery was eradicated,
And I don't need to be validated.
I need you to understand about the
Residual effects of slavery,
And believe me when I tell you that systemic racism exists.
Disparities in education, health, and wealth.
Slaves forbidden to learn to read or write.
Poorly fed and overworked.
No healthcare.
Cramped living quarters with no room to spare.
Emancipated with no wealth, no help
And Black codes to keep them in check.
What do you expect?
Sherman's Field Order No. 15
Forty acres and a mule
One of the first of many broken promises.
The truth is cruel.
After over two hundred years of free labor,
We were set free to fend for ourselves,
While White people retained their wealth.

Restitution to African Americans for enslavement was a lie.
To make matters worse,
Every time we rise on our feet,
You change the rules of engagement,
But we will not retreat.
Though we are knocked down again and again
Through various forms of oppression —
Inequitable school funding
Voter suppression
School-to-prison pipeline
Housing loans declined.
Fatal police shootings of unarmed Blacks.
Longer prison sentences for Black men
For the same crimes committed as Whites.
Job and housing discrimination.
Those are the facts.

Connor

Everybody has their struggles,
But you can't blame everything on the past.
If you commit a crime,
You have to be prepared to do the time.
It doesn't matter what color you are.
You can't go around breaking the law,
And then blame the system or get mad with the judge
For doing his job.
Because Your Honor
Didn't fall for a sad sob
Story about how your daddy abandoned the family
And your mama got hooked on crack.

That's not systemic racism.

Those are — as you said in your own words — the facts.

What about DNA evidence exonerating innocent Black men

Who went to prison because an unreliable witness

Placed them at the scene of the crime

Even when they had an alibi for their time.

Or what about cops and prosecutors withholding evidence

That could prove a man's innocence,

But because of the color of his skin,

He's found guilty. That's what I call filthy.

They go on with their lives.

He goes to prison.

Systemic racism wins.

Tayvion

Some bruhs aren't lucky enough to make it to the Pen.

Like Michael Brown

Who was gunned down,

Not by Bloods or Crips.

No, it was the Five-O who tripped

Because the dude and his friend were walking in the street

Instead of on the sidewalk

Shots fired.

Michael Brown goes down.

Officers swore it wasn't their fault.

A simple case of self-defense

Witnesses disagreed

Hence protests commenced

After Michael's body lay dead in the street
For four hours while his grandmother wept.
Officials telling the Black community to just chill
Like that's supposed to be cool
Yes, this made our people livid at the boys in the blue.
The community responded like a woman scorned,
Our faith in the justice system severed and torn.

Connor

Smashing car windows,
Looting items from stores,
Protesters standing on police cars,
Businesses burned to the ground
Damaged or destroyed.
Molotov cocktails thrown at police.
Those weren't peaceful protesters.
Those were thugs.

Ladarius

There will always be some angry protesters
That will respond with violence,
To police killings of unarmed Blacks,
So don't expect the unrest to cease.
No justice. No peace.
What about the peaceful protesters
Who were greeted by police in riot gear,
Carrying assault rifles and shields?
Protesters sprayed with tear gas, clutching their eyes in fear.
Rubber bullets fired into the crowd.
Children holding their ears.

Weapons pointed at them.
This should never have been allowed.
Defund the Police

Jasmine

I support defunding the police.
Reduce police budgets.
It's not as if crime is getting any better
With more police officers on the beat.
All they do is cause more grief.
Blacks in the US are three times more likely to be killed by police.

Hunter

Defunding the police is a dumb idea.
People are going to break the law
If there is no one there to keep them in line.
If you defund the police, who's going to fight crime?

Jamir

I say dude has been watching too much of *The Purge*.
Law-abiding citizens aren't suddenly gonna have the urge
To go on a killing spree.
That's television. We're talking about reality.
Community Policing

Zaquaisha

I'm in favor of community policing.
Let's build a bridge, not a wall.
United we stand. Divided we fall,
Right?

My uncle is Five-O.
The people in his community know him,
And he knows them.

Jamarcus

Your uncle might be on the up.
No disrespect,
But the police are the ones who need a foot on their neck.
I don't trust them anymore.
Police are more violent than before.

Jamir

Bruh, police brutality ain't nothing new.
What about Rodney King and the LA riots in 1992?
Watching video of King being struck
More than fifty times with batons
And kicked was mad crazy.

Emma

You're forgetting about safety.
King was driving over a hundred miles per hour
While intoxicated. Dude was faded.

DeAndre

So, I guess the savage beating the officers gave King demonstrated
What happens when you get caught DUI
Or should I say DWB?
King was unarmed.

Hunter

They stopped a reckless man from causing serious harm
To other drivers and pedestrians,
But I guess you overlooked that detail,
That's not the only thing you failed
To mention, like the fact
That King led the cops on a high-speed chase,
And resisted arrest.

Jasmine

According to who — the same police officers
Who used a stun gun to burn a hole in his chest,
Fractured his cheekbone, before his arrest
Caused nearly a dozen injuries to his skull,
And gave him a broken leg
And threw a sheet over his head after beating him half-dead,
And then lied
Saying King received only minor injuries
And their actions justified,
Saying that he should have complied.
But the video told a different story.
Backed into a corner, the LA district attorney
Had no other choice
But to charge the officers with use of excessive force,
Knowing all along that they would be acquitted.

Fajah

Well-stated.

Connor

King's injuries were exaggerated.

Fajah

King suffered the rest of his life because of the injuries he sustained
He lived in constant pain.
Those officers deserved to go to prison,
Instead, they got to go home to their families,
That's what American justice looks like.
That's the difference between Black and White.

Khalan

And that's why you had the LA riots.

Caroline

Watts, LA, Ferguson. Is that the only way you know
How to respond is with violence?

Khalan

When you slap cops on the wrists,
We respond with our fists.
You call it violence. Man, y'all really trying it.
We see it as a way to get your attention,
A way for our voices to be heard.

Emma

That's absurd.
You think resorting to violence
And burning down buildings will bring about change.
You are going about it all wrong.

You can't use brute force to make people
Behave differently, like you're King Kong.

DeAndre

Why not? Isn't that what the colonists did to the slaves?

Caroline

Am I dreaming, or are we back on slavery again?
It's like a nightmare that never ends.

Jaquesha

Yes, we are back on slavery again.
Apparently, you didn't get the memo
Just so you know,
Our assignment is about CRT.
Which has been impacted by the institution of slavery.

Me

Imagine running a race, but your competitors
Are near the finish line when you take off from the starting line.
How can you possibly make up for lost time?
That's what slavery did to the Black race.
It put us behind.
Allow me to explain.
Three men run away from a cruel taskmaster,
A Dutchman, a Scotchman, and an African.
All three are caught.
Imagine you are the African.
Your heart pounds furiously
As you stand before a board of all White men.

Your ebony skin
Stands out like a fly in a glass of milk.
Beads of sweat form on your crinkled forehead
And began slowly trickling down your face
As you await your fate.
The hairs on the back of your neck stand on end.
Will you be made to return to the plantation
From which you escaped?
You glance over at your master.
The veins in his neck stand out in livid ridges.
His mouth tightens into a stubborn line.
A sickening wave of terror wells up in your belly
As the board announces their ruling.
What is the punishment when freedom is your crime?
All three men are to receive thirty lashes of the whip.
The Dutchman and the Scotchman receive a one-year extension
To their indentured servitude and an additional three years
Of servitude to the colony,
Then they turn to you, you feel the hostility.
Your crime was no greater and no less than the other men
Involved in the conspiracy,
Yet the court sentences you to serve your master
For the rest of your natural life.
Disparity grips your soul.
Your knees buckle as your fate sinks in — life without parole.

Khalan

Black people worked your fields.

Connor

And my people in return provided room and board and gave them free meals.

Khalan

You raped us of our culture and denied us the right to be a part of yours.

Connor

You were heathens, barbarians, running around naked in the jungle. We made you a civilized people.

Khalan

Says the dude wearing Goth eyeliner and matching black hair
And enough body piercings to bleed out.
It's obvious that you're no boy scout.
But tell me this,
What is more barbaric than kidnapping a man
From the only home he has ever known,
Placing him in chains, changing his name,
And taking away his freedom of choice?
Stripping him of his native identity
Taking away his right to be free
Selling people like livestock,
Separating parents and children,
Referring to people as personal property.
Making them think that they should be grateful
To the master for giving them a shanty for a shelter
Like they've won the lottery.

Connor

It couldn't have been all that bad.

After slaves were set free,

Many of them returned to the plantation.

That's where they were most happy.

DeAndre

Sorry for your misinformation.

But it didn't mean that the slaves were happy

As slaves.

It only meant that they learned how to

Survive in their situation.

That's what we do as Black people.

We learn to adapt.

That's a useful survival skill

Until it becomes a trap.

That's right. It can become a trap.

We adapt, and we conform

Until it becomes the norm,

Systemic racism has become the norm.

Jackson

Let your pain bring about change.

You people are always looking for someone to blame.

It is so convenient to blame your economic situation

On discrimination.

Ladarius

Let's not forget that it was your people who brought my people over here in chains.

Hadley

I'm sorry for what happened,
I didn't create the problem.
I inherited it just like the rest of you.
You want to shame us
And blame us.
Force us to feel guilty about the past
Because we are White.
That's not right.

Jamarcus

We don't have to take it back to slavery or the Trail of Tears.
Let's talk about what's happened in recent years.
Police Killing Unarmed Blacks
George Floyd — a knee to the neck.
Racial tensions
The domino effect.
Protests and marches
To raise awareness
About inequities
In our criminal justice system.
You dismissed him
Like a piece of lint,
But like the others, he meant
Something to someone.
His life mattered,
When you took it, you shattered
A family, bereaved a community,
Thinking your uniform gave you immunity
But we came out in record numbers

To say Black Lives Matter.

Emma

Once again, you're making this about race.

Are you forgetting the reason why

The police were called to that location in the first place.

George Floyd had committed a crime.

Videos aren't always reliable.

First, we were told that Chauvin was on Floyd's neck eight min forty-six seconds.

Now, they're saying it was nine minutes and twenty-nine seconds.

Which is it?

Who changed the time?

Fajah

Emma, you must be outta your mind.

Who cares about the time?

Is eight mins and forty-six seconds not long enough to do the job?

Maybe Floyd had a fake twenty.

I don't know,

But he didn't rob a bank.

What about all those white-collar crimes,

Like embezzlement and stock manipulation,

That carry less time than street crimes?

The crimes your kind commit and get away with.

And when they are convicted,

They get a trip to a dope country club prison.

How's that for punishment?

Meanwhile Black justice is almost nonexistent.

Caroline

You're so busy pointing fingers. You don't know who to blame.
You expect police officers to do the job of politicians,
And politicians to make decisions
That support your assertion that everybody is working
To get the Black man down.

Tayvion

If that's not true, explain voter suppression
Gerrymandering,
Restricting voting access.
Sounds familiar?
Voter registration literacy test.
We want a fair and free election,
But what we're getting are more restrictive voting laws
To keep us from going to the polls.

Emma

If you believe that you are victims, then you are a victim
It's all a state of mind.
If you are looking for excuses, they aren't hard to find.
But if you want to achieve the American dream,
Then you have to set the bar high.
Run, walk, crawl, climb
Do whatever it takes.
It's all a state of mind.

Systematic Inequality

Me

You say that systematic inequality is all a state of mind,

That we're not trying

Hard enough to achieve the American dream.

Did you ever have to run, walk, crawl, or climb just to be seen?

No. That's because equality is your American birthright,

Unfortunately, I have a different plight

I can be honest and yet treated like a thief.

I can struggle to breathe but receive no relief.

I can come in peace and be confronted with hostility.

I can plant roots in my community

But feel no stability.

I can commit the same or lesser crimes as Whites but serve more time.

I can be more qualified and still denied

Employment, bonuses, raises, and promotions.

I can break into a convenience store

And go away for a long time,

But a White person can break into the Capitol

And be home by dinnertime.

DeAndre

What if the rioters that attacked the Capitol

And threatened the lives of lawmakers on January 6 had been Black?

Ladarius

Hundreds of dead Black bodies inside the Capitol and on the grounds.

Not enough body bags to go around.

Domestic Terrorism

Me

QAnon

Proud Boys

Right Wing Death Squad.

A hangman's noose on the Capitol's grounds,

But no one thought that was odd

Behavior that warranted the National Guard.

They broke through barricades,

Assaulted police,

Smashed windows and doors,

Stormed the halls of Congress

Interrupting a joint session

Of Congress

To overturn America's presidential election.

They walked through the halls of the Capitol

Carrying Confederate flags,

They entered Senate chambers,

Kicked up their feet,

Even stopped to smoke weed.

We all saw the images. We all watched the videos.

We saw the difference in the responses to BLM protesters

And White boys gone wild in the capitol.

Now do you still believe CRT has no merit,

Or do you finally get it?

Hunter

Okay, so a few boneheads screwed up royally,

You cut off dead branches to save a tree.

What they did had nothing to do with CRT.
You keep talking about systemic racism.
You want to cancel culture,
Destroy the legacy of great men,
Portray them as villains
When they were willing to give their lives
For this nation.
That should give you an indication
Of the kind of people they were.
You can't cancel culture.
You can't erase history
Or challenge its validity.

Zaquaisha

We are not trying to erase or rewrite history.
We're asking America to fix mistakes of the past,
That can be corrected,
By tearing down statues that were erected
In honor of men who believed in and fought to preserve
The institution of slavery.
We are asking America to tell the truth about our country's history —
The good and the bad
So we can learn from the past and move forward,
So that the next generation of Blacks do not have to plead
With America to be treated equally.

Khalan

I want equality too, but as long as it is just us,
There will be no justice.

Javier

Blacks are not the only ones who experience racial biases.
Try thinking about someone putting up a wall to keep you out
Or putting you in cages once you're in the United States.

Jackson

Africans were brought here against their will,
But you sneak across the border and then complain.
If you hate it here, you can always go back to Mexico.

Javier

I'm from El Salvador.
My parents left their country because of gang warfare.
It was much too dangerous for them to stay there,
But I don't owe you an explanation.
You don't own America.
You don't own this nation.

Dual Citizenship

Kabria

I listened to those who believe CRT explains systemic racism,
And I listened to those who believe CRT is being used
As an excuse for failure.
I'm not going to choose sides.
I'm not going to offer a compromise,
But since I hold dual citizenship, I think I can speak
Without being biased.
CRT is Black people's reality,
While cancel culture is White people's
Connection to their "proud" history.

White America

Kabria

White America — you can't throw a rock and hide your hand.
You brought enslaved Africans to this land.
You removed Native Americans from their homes
And put them on reservations.
You worked Chinese immigrants for low wages
And poor accommodations.
You created Black codes and segregated laws,
Laying the foundation for a system
That oppresses people of color.
You wove racism into the fabric of this nation.
Now you're attempting to silence those
Who are expressing their frustration,
Who are demanding real change
From institutions,
Real changes in policies and laws
That are severely structurally flawed.
Systemic racism is real
And America can never heal
If we pretend systemic racism doesn't exist,
And defend or justify our treatment
Of her Brown and Black citizens.

Black America

Kabria

Black America, people of color,

You can't live with a victim mentality

Even though systemic racism is a reality,

Instead of complaining about not getting a break,

Try owning up to your mistakes

Everything that happens to you is not the White man's fault.

You have a responsibility to your own destiny.

Stop saying that nothing has changed.

That is not true.

Slavery was abolished.

Segregation ended

Voter rights established

A Black president elected.

Progress reflected

Yes, America defaulted on its promise,

But you inherited more than a legacy of slavery.

You inherited a legacy of bravery,

Determination

And faith.

The Black part of me is just as tired of racism

As the rest of you

And the White part of me

Wants to know what I can do

To fix the problem.

I realize that it's going to take a joint effort,

Just like it did to abolish slavery,

And end segregation.

Like it or not, we are one nation.
If we are going to put an end to systemic racism,
We must acknowledge its existence
And work together to change policies and systems
That breathe life into it,
And I, personally, believe we can do it.

Be Their Voice

Ms. Jordan looks around the room.
Her eyes glisten.
Her lips curve slightly upward.
Her palms clap together like crashing cymbals.
We are proud of ourselves.
Maybe some of us will never agree on CRT,
but at least we know where each other stand and why.
We tackled a tough issue,
argued our differences,
and demystified systemic racism.
I hang around after class
until the last
student leaves.

I wait around to ask Ms. Jordan
what made her decide to let us battle rap in class.
She said she saw me battling rap at the park
    and was impressed that "after ARGUING YOUR POINTS,
you gave one another fist and shoulder bumps."

I explain the only people that get into fights after battle raps are chumps.
Bars can be brutal, but they aren't meant to be taken literal.
This ain't like no East Coast–West Coast feud,
if there was such a thing.
Point is. You leave it on the stage,
whether you win or lose.
Ms. Jordan says she liked what she saw
and thought it might work for the poetry class, and it did.

She thought outside the box. Sometimes to reach students,
you got to go off the grid.
Ms. Jordan says I made her a better teacher.
The truth is she made me more than a better poet.
She made me a better person.
My first impression of Ms. Jordan was wrong.
She was the right instructor for the class.
As I'm telling Ms. Jordan what a dope teacher she is,
She tells me she has a favor to ask.
"I need a speaker to talk about
                    our city's CURRENT RACIAL CLIMATE
at a residential community meeting
in a predominantly White suburb.
They are disturbed
by what's happening in our city and are interested
in learning what can be done to improve race relations."
Ms. Jordan says she'd like to recommend me as the guest speaker
because I know what it feels like to be a
                    VICTIM OF POLICE BRUTALITY.
"You know what it would take to make you feel safe," she says.
"I don't think they are holding a community meeting
because they are concerned about my safety," I reply.
"Maybe not." Ms. Jordan nods. "But your safety is important,
and they need to know that."
"Don't expect them to roll out the welcome mat."
"So, you'll do it?" she says.
"Yes," I reply, "but only on one condition.
You can't tell them who I am before the meeting.
                    They'll just PREJUDGE me.
That will defeat the mission."

Ms. Jordan agrees and hands me a slip of paper
with the date and address.
There is just one other problem.
The community meeting is the same day as the BLM protest
at City Hall.
I have an obligation to my mama and my community to be there.
They are all counting on me to tell MY STORY.
Ms. Jordan thanks me again.
I turn to walk away, but my feet are glued to the floor.
I tell her that I had nothing to do with the school riot,
but I know some guys that were a part of it,
and they're not hard-core.
They're not different from me. They made a bad choice.
Ms. Jordan pats my hand and says,
"Mason, when you speak at the community meeting
and at City Hall,
BE THEIR VOICE."

I can't wait to get home to tell Mama what happened in poetry class.
She listens with a warm smile on her face,
the smile that tells me she is really proud of me.
"Mason, do you know why I protest?" she asks.
"I think so," I say.
"To make my voice heard," she says.
"That's what the BLM protest is about,
making our voices heard.
We want to send a message to every attorney general,
every prosecutor, and every grand jury that we demand justice.
That we will not be deterred.
The victims can't speak for themselves.

We must speak for them.
        It is important THAT WE BE THEIR VOICE."

For the first time since taking poetry class,
I am really looking forward to going to class.
Everyone has been pretty cool,
even Hunter isn't his usual obnoxious self.
As Ms. Jordan is reading a poem she wrote,
Principal Martin knocks on the door,
whispers something in Ms. Jordan's ear.
She collapses onto the floor
after learning her father has died of a stroke.

The poetry class writes cards and sends flowers and letters,
anything to make Ms. Jordan feel better.
For two weeks, we endure her replacement,
a retired English teacher
with as much charm as a Tasmanian devil.
Two weeks feels like forever.
When Ms. Jordan returns, she isn't herself,
like a piece of her was left in the town
she used to call home.
Rumors surface that her father stopped speaking
to her when she adopted a Black child
and that her husband left her for someone else.
Every day, a little bit of Ms. Jordan diminishes.
Students and teachers are whispering
that she looks thin and pale.
I can't help but notice that she is the shell
of the person she used to be.

I want to be there for her, like she has been there for me,
for us — her students.
I hang around after class. "Ms. Jordan, can I talk to you?" I ask.
"You got so much pain bottled up inside,
but that's not the place where it belongs.
No one has a perfect life and even roses have thorns."
Ms. Jordan thanks me as I leave.
I have no idea if what I said made a difference.

The next day, she announces that she wants to share
a poem she wrote called "The Inheritance."

The Inheritance

I did not bother to attend the reading
of the will, for I knew the contents thereof.
I had been disinherited long ago.
Only yesterday, he had been laid to rest,
but I had been dead to him for seventeen years.
His words are as acidic now as they were then.
"You have ruined the family's name
and brought shame
upon us in that you insisted on adopting a Black child.
I cannot be angry with you because
God has not allowed you to bear me an heir,
but I can with justifiable indignation
be furious with you for electing to adopt a child
that is a total embarrassment.
to our family's great name,
yet I am not totally without blame.
For I knew when you brought a Black classmate home
from college that you had changed,
but your digression is far greater than I ever imagined.
How shall we ever hold our heads up again in this town?
Seeing that you have chosen this child over your family,
as of this day, you are no longer my daughter.
I have removed you from my will."
I had no choice but to accept my father's
wishes to alienate me.
From that moment, time stood still.
Although I was not bothered by my child's race,
it was painful knowing that I would never again

see my father's face.
He was a man of his word and had vowed
to never speak to me again.
I died a thousand deaths
when I heard of his failing health
and longed to reconcile with him,
not to have my name reinstated in his will
but to tell him that I loved him still.
He refused to see me, to speak with me.
I was counted as a stranger in his eyes.
He had severed the ties,
never to be mended,
forever broken fences.

———

"I'm sorry that your father couldn't see beyond race," says Javier.
"What you did — adopting that child — was really cool."
"Thank you, Javier," says Ms. Jordan.

After Ms. Jordan shared her truth, there was an atmospheric shift.
We had been like boats adrift
that were finally on course to our destination — CHANGE.
Not only changes in our community but changes in us.

Be the Change

Ms. Jordan is a lot like my mama — strong when she has to be
and soft when she needs to be.
Ms. Jordan's bravery gives me confidence
I need to get back involved in the BLM movement.
Today is my first BLM protest since my RUN-IN WITH POLICE.
Today is different.

Today people are CHANTING MY NAME.

BLM demonstrators
walking in the footsteps of Dr. King.
Nonviolent resistance.
Violence approaching in the distance.
The Extremes marching with Neo-Confederate,
Nazi, and American flags,
shouting that they're taking their country back.
Hunter Abbott at the demonstration hiding behind the scenes.
Not marching with the Extremes.
Other hate groups in the midst.
The police are here too.
Sultan, Jay D, and Kaesan trying their best to keep their cool.
It's hard not to react
to racial slurs and venomous words
coming from counterprotesters.

Diamond is at the rally.
"What are you doing here?" she asks.
"If you want change, you got to be the change, right?"
"I was worried about you," says Diamond.
"You could have called," I say.

"I'm sorry. I just assumed it was too soon."

"It doesn't matter now." I shrug.

"Mason, you don't have anything to prove."

"Is that why you think I'm here, to prove something to you?"

Diamond doesn't have a clue.

The BLM movement is bigger than any one person.

"That's not what I said," she responds, raising her voice.

"You didn't have to." I blow a deep breath.

I had ESCAPED DEATH.

Unlike some BLM victims.

So why should I have to explain why I came

to support the cause.

Diamond's hand touches my shoulder.

I pause,

then pull away.

"I never meant to offend you," she says, determined

to finish the conversation we started.

I raise my hand for her to keep quiet.

People are staring at us.

We are here for a protest, not a RIOT.

"My mom's up next," I tell her.

Mama walks up on the platform

and turns to the crowd.

Loud enough but not too loud

to make her come off as just another angry Black mom

who didn't teach her son how to respect the police.

The Sequel

We like to think
that it's only troublemakers
who have run-ins with the law,
but Mason is no troublemaker.
He's a high school senior.
He makes decent grades.
He don't give me an ounce of trouble.
I taught him to steer clear of trouble.
That's what he was doing that day
when the police stopped him.
He was staying out of trouble
but somehow trouble found him.
Mason could have participated
in that school riot,
but he didn't.
He went to class.
That video is a mother's worst nightmare.
Mason lived
because he had a community
that came to his aid.
Had he been alone,
I might have been at a funeral today
instead of here speaking to you.
His physical wounds are healing,
but his nerves are still reeling.
You don't walk away
from something like that unscathed.
As a mother I am outraged

about what happened to my son.
I'd like to say that it could happen to anyone,
but for some reason or other,
it keeps happening to Black people.
Some call it a coincidence.
I call it an unending sequel.

———

"Your mom was good."

"Nah. Let's get it straight.

My mama was better than good. She was great."

"Okay. Okay." Diamond grins.

"You're smiling. I guess that means we're still friends."

"Sure." I shrug.

"About earlier, I'm sorry," Diamond replies with regret in her eyes.

"We straight," I said.

She appears relieved.

"Is it strange hearing people chant your name?"

"That's why I'm wearing this fitted."

"With all these people here," Diamond looks around,

"someone's bound to recognize you as the guy

who got beat up by the police."

"I don't care that people know what happened to me.

I just don't want to make it all about me.

I survived. A lot of VICTIMS OF POLICE BRUTALITY did not."

"Survivor's guilt?" Diamond asks.

"No. I don't feel guilty that my mama didn't have to bury me

or sit through court hearings

or have to spend her Sunday afternoons at the cemetery.

We all know that these MARCHES ARE NECESSARY.

I just don't want people to get so caught up in hashtags

and chanting names that they forget what we are really doing out here.

It's about change. No, it's more than that.

It's about being the change.

Speaking of that, I got somewhere I need to be."

"You got a battle rap coming up?"

"SOMETHING LIKE THAT."

"Something like that?" Diamond repeats my words

like she's about to give me the third degree.

"You wanna come with me?" I ask.

"No," she chuckles. "I told you rapping isn't my thing,"

I lean in and whisper in her ear, "Maybe next time."

"Don't count on it." Diamond presses her lips into a fine line.

I give her deuces. "Peace out," I say.

She returns a Mona Lisa smile.

Just as I am leaving,

a car plows through the crowd.

People flying into the air.

Blood spatter like graffiti covering the streets.

Dozens placed in ambulances. Two covered in white sheets.

Driver abandons the car, fleeing the scene.

Officials call it the work of a lone offender.

We know it's the work of the Extremes.

Domestic terrorism no longer a threat.

Police say they're widening their dragnet

which is suspect

since racist manifestos are often posted online.

I guess violence against Blacks don't count as a crime.

But I got to hold on to the belief that mentality will change.

I've seen Whites bleed and Blacks bleed.

The color of our blood is the same.
A voice tells me to go home.
It's not safe to be out here walking alone,
but if I don't go and make my voice heard,
those BLM protesters will have died in vain.
The fact remains that if you want to see change,
you got to be that change you want to see.

Battle Rap Challenge

I'm two blocks from the spot
where Ms. Jordan told me to meet her
when I see Jontrae heading my way.
We haven't spoken in a minute.
We ain't never been tight,
but rappers maintain a mutual respect for the craft.
We may diss one another during a battle rap,
but if the other is drowning,
we'll throw out the life raft.
Jontrae wants to know if I'm ready
for another drop-the-mic
or if I'm running scared?
He tells me that Tony is hosting a battle rap in two weeks.
I heard about it, but I haven't signed up for the contest.
He says the winner is gonna walk away with two grand,
then he tells me that is chump change for him
and that he was just looking out for me.

I tell him that I got something bigger going on.
He wants to know what could be bigger than Tony's Drop-the-Mic,
so I tell him two people were fatally hit by a car at the BLM march today
and that I got to be there for the cause.
Jontrae takes a moment to pause
and say that's bad what happened to the demonstrators,
but some big wheels in the industry are coming to Tony's Drop-the-Mic
and that's an opportunity for me to get my name out there.

I tell Jontrae that I'd love to drop the mic on him,

but I gotta come up with some lyrics to rap about
what's happening in our community,
our country.
I tell him Martin's dream is ours now.
I thought life was all about rapping,
but some brothers just want to survive a traffic stop
or make it home to their families
when they're confronted by a cop.

I gotta be at the BLM protest,
but I wish Jontrae the best.
He tells me to do what I gotta do.
He gives me deuces before walking away.
Ms. Jordan is waiting for me at the library
with a distorted look on her face.
She heard about the violence
that erupted at the BLM march
and asks if I want to cancel the presentation.
I keep it on the real.
The image of body bags has me shook.
You'd think that after nearly being killed
by the police while walking home from the park
and after witnessing a peaceful protest turn deadly
that I'd be ready to concede,
but justice has become the air I breathe.
"I got this," I tell her.
Admiring my BLM pullover and freshly retwisted locks,
she says I look nice, then glances at her watch.
"They like starting on time."
"I know. We are not on CPT," I say.

"What?"

"Colored People Time."

"I know what it means.

That phrase is meant to be racist by design," she says.

Ms. Jordan looks as if she's about to hurl.

"It's okay, Ms. Jordan. I'm only messing with your head."

She nods and offers a faint smile.

We climb into her car and travel
to the other side of the world.

The Other World

I wonder if Ms. Jordan is more nervous about having a
young Black man in her car.
I resist the urge to ask how far
we have to travel.
She senses what I'm thinking
and tells me that we're going to Bellevue,
which is only about five miles away.
I've never been to Bellevue.
I've only passed by there,
but you'd have to live under a rock
not to have heard of Bellevue,
the envy of the Hamptons.
The mayor of Pendleton lives there.
He never comes down
from his ivory tower
to talk to the people in the communities he serves,
so how could he relate
to what's happening beyond the gate?
We ride in complete silence
until we arrive at our destination.
I can feel Ms. Jordan's hesitation,
but it's too late.
She puts in a code.
We enter their world.
Ms. Jordan pulls into a reserved parking space.
"Wait in the car. I'll call you when they're ready."
She squeezes my hand then goes inside the building.
I wait in the parking lot until she signals me.

Community Meeting

I join Ms. Jordan at the front of the room.
Mouths agape,
angry scowls.
Loud whispers
coming from the small crowd.
The room grows still,
as silent as the tomb,
sucking air out of me like a vacuum.
Their eyes are judging me,
my hair, the color of my skin,
the BLM hoodie I'm wearing.

If You Knew My Name

Me

Good afternoon.
My name is Mason Zy'Aire Tyndall.
From the looks on your faces,
you seem very disappointed.
Perhaps you were expecting
someone in a suit and tie,
with a classic taper haircut and ivory skin,
not a Black male in a hoodie, with dreads and ebony skin.
I asked Ms. Jordan not to reveal my identity.
I did not want to be prejudged,
so, I have to ask,
if you knew my name,
would you have rescinded your invitation?
Would you have required an explanation
from Ms. Jordan
as to why I was chosen to be your speaker?
If you knew my name
would you be eager to hear what I have to say,
or would you cry foul play?
If my name was Seth, Liam, Dylan, Hunter, or Grayson
and not Hakeem, Tyquan, DeAndre, Zy'Aire, or Mason
would you have done a double take,
or would you have extended me a friendly handshake?
Expectations — we all have them.
Disappointments — we all get them.
When you look like me, you get them a lot.
I was taught from the time I was big enough to walk

that this is the land of the free (just not for me)
and the home of the brave.
It's hard to feel brave when you're afraid
that you might not live to see another day.
That's how I felt as I lay on the pavement.
Beaten, kicked,
feeling sick to my stomach.
In an instance, my self-esteem plummeted.
I went from feeling like I was on top of the world
to feeling like the world was on top of me.
That scene plays over and over in my head.
The gun pointed at me,
my eyes closed.
Thinking okay. This is it. I'm dead.
I remember his blue uniform.
His badge number, the death stare,
feelings of despair.
Becoming the latest hashtag.
A few days later standing in the school assembly
asked to salute the flag,
in honor of a country
that does not protect me.

Police Officer

I will be first to tell you
that the criminal justice system is not perfect,
but I swore to serve and protect,
and I take those duties seriously.
You have a right to be angry,
but it's not a fair assessment to say

that all officers are the same
and that we should all bear the blame
for police violence.
There are officers who make errors in judgment.
There are officers that need sensitivity training,
and then there are some bad cops
that slipped through the cracks.
I can't make excuses for them.
The facts are the facts,
but to say that the entire criminal justice system
is out to get Blacks is just not true.

Me

Tell me that when you are handcuffed
with a gun pointed at your head.
Tell me that when you see the stats
and you realize that you have a greater chance
of going to jail than college,
and no one seems to want to acknowledge
that what's happening to the Black community
is a big deal,
that systemic racism is real.
I was at a peaceful protest today that turned violent
because there are still people that want to keep us silent.
Growing up, my mom would tell me
about the 1992 LA riot.
I cringed when I saw the videotape of four White officers
savagely beating and kicking
an unarmed Black guy squirming on the ground
as their brothers in uniform watched,

appearing callously nonchalant.
An LA city councilmember gave a possible explanation
for their behaviors, he said,
"The first way to open the door
to brutalizing people in any place
is to cheapen their worth as human beings."
From the slave market
to the job market,
the worth of Blacks has been cheapened
to the point that we feel as if we have to remind you
that our lives matter.

Community Resident

When I see you, I don't see color.

Me

You can't dismiss my skin color.
That won't make the problem go away.
Unconscious biases — we all have them.
A Black man driving a Benz must be dealing drugs.
Young Black men wearing hoodies must be thugs.
It would be nice if I could go places
and not have to think about skin color or race,
but in my world, microaggressions are commonplace.
And so is violence against people of color
by the men and women in blue.
If this were an isolated few,
perhaps then you could make a persuasive argument
that there is no cause for alarm.
I cannot tell you the number of times

I've heard my mother pray
or seen my mother cry
because another Black family was forced to say goodbye
to a loved one gunned down,
or airway restricted
because he was placed in handcuffs face down on the ground
or held in a deadly chokehold
by the people sworn to protect
who instead use their power to control.
Like the aftermath of a tornado, they leave families
and communities devastated.
Public officials offer condolences,
stating the incident will be investigated.
Words console,
but until Black lives matter
to more than just Black people,
this chain of events will continue to unfold.

Community Resident

We are not trying to dismiss anyone. That's why we brought you here
today, to talk about what's happening in our city. We did not know
that the speaker was going to be Black, only that someone would come
in to talk to us about our current racial climate.

Me

It's difficult to address our current racial climate
without acknowledging how we arrived at this point
and the progress we've made.
During emancipation, the nation was compelled to accept
that no man had a right to own another man.

And so the master released his slave.
That was a step in the right direction.
During the Civil Rights Movement,
the nation was compelled to accept that separate
but equal was not just,
another step in the right direction,
but that's not enough.

Community Resident

The wheels of justice turn slowly, but they do turn.

Me

That's easy to say when you live behind a secured gate,
but when you're walking home, and you're stopped
and get the crap beat out of you by cops,
you fear that justice may someday come too late.

Community Resident

We are doing our best to understand the Black community and their
interactions with police. We would like the violence to cease. We're
afraid of what will happen if it continues.

Me

You are afraid that the burning
and looting will reach your community,
that your gates no longer provide immunity.
As long as you view the world as us and them,
you will always condemn
our quest for equality,
partly because you cannot relate

to the frustration we feel

when we are treated as if our lives do not matter.

The quest for justice is a never-ending chapter.

If you truly want to understand the Black community,

I invite you to attend a BLM rally,

meet with residents in our community,

talk to us, listen to us, ask us why we are so angry.

"The Negro community is about to reach a breaking point.

There is a great deal of frustration and despair

and confusion in the Negro community,

and there is a feeling of being alone and not feeling protected.

If you walk the street, you aren't safe.

If you're at home, you aren't safe.

So that the Negro feels that everywhere he goes . . .

he's in danger of some physical violence."

These words were spoken by Dr. King in 1963.

Why should they still apply to me?

If I walk the street, I am not safe.

If I am at home, I am not safe.

I will never feel safe

as long as racial equality is a wish list

and racial disparities persist

and justice applies, just not for me.

Community Resident

Mason, thank you for coming. You have enlightened us today. We
are hopeful that we will be able to come together with the Black
community and the police department, and unify our city.

Police Officer

I look forward to meeting with your community leaders to build
better relationships with the Black community.

The officer shakes my hand and offers an apology
on the behalf of the police department.
I accept his apology and extend a personal invitation
for him to join me at the next protest rally. He says that he will attend.

The mayor of Pendleton and other prominent community figures
met with BLM leaders.
My mama was one of the leaders that sat down with them.
After that, the looting stopped. That wasn't the only thing that changed.
After the classroom battle rap, the poetry class
talked more about poetry and less about racial issues in our city.
Maybe we just needed to deal with the elephant in the room.
It sure felt good writing about beauty for a change
after talking so much about pain.
I was excited about what was happening in my city,
in my community, in my poetry class,
but there was one more thing I had to do —
the BLM rally.
I realize I have a gift, and it isn't for me to prove
that I am better at rapping than Nimrod or earn Hitman's respect.
I was the Black man down on the ground,
a message I must reflect.

BLM Rally

Ms. Jordan greets me at the BLM rally with a smile so wide
I can see her molars.
Ms. Franklin, the school counselor,
and the officer from the Bellevue community meeting
and Diamond are here.
They are all here.
They are here because they believe
that better race relations are not only possible;
they are also necessary.

Real change isn't FRAGMENTARY.

That's what we experienced in the past,
but now we are learning to work in harmony.

I feel a gentle hand touch my shoulder.
It is Diamond.
The wallflower is getting bolder.
"I've been thinking about what you told me
about how I should enjoy my senior year.
I've been so busy thinking about my future career,

that I've been MISSING OUT on this part of my life.

My studies are important, but so is hanging out with friends.
Do you want to hang out sometimes?" Diamond asks.
"That all depends
on your definition of having fun," I reply.
"A movie, pizza."
"Sounds good, but I need to holla at Ms. Franklin.
I'll catch up with you later?"
"Okayyy." Diamond scratches the back of her neck.

"Did you just blow off Diamond?" Ms. Franklin asks.

"She studies a lot, but THERE IS MORE TO HER than her books."

"If I didn't know any better, Ms. Franklin,

I'd think you were trying to get me a hook up."

Ms. Franklin chuckles. "I'm no matchmaker."

"What you are is a great school counselor."

"I heard you are doing well in the Black poetry class."

"Yeah, I'm maintaining an A."

"From what Ms. Jordan tells me, it is a well-deserved A."

"Thanks for talking me into taking it."

"Do you still want to be a rapper?

"Yes, ma'am."

"Let me know when you have your first concert, I'll be there."

"Somehow, I can't imagine you at a rap concert," I tell Ms. Franklin.

"Never JUDGE A BOOK by its cover.

The more you learn, the more you will discover

that things aren't always as they appear."

"I'll try to remember that," I reply.

"I have something for you."

Ms. Franklin reaches into her jacket pocket and hands me a CD.

My brows snap together. "What's this?"

"A little OLD SKOOL something," she says.

I know Ms. Franklin. There's got to be a twist.

"She kinda looks like you," I say.

"Oh snap. That is you, Ms. Franklin. You were a rapper!"

"KC Key."

"My mom has some of your CDs. I ain't never heard her play them,

but I've seen them in her CD collection."

"All three of them."

"What happened? Why did you stop rappin'?"

"I had my reasons at the time. It doesn't matter now.

I love what I do, guiding MISDIRECTED missiles like you."

"You are good at your job," I say, thinking about the day we first met.

"You know I don't expect to pay for those tickets, right?"

Ms. Franklin peers over her glasses.

"Ms. Franklin, when I make it big, you get front row seats and backstage passes."

"Mason, are you ready?" a protest leader interrupts.

"I'm ready," I answer.

Black Lives State of Mind

The music's thumping. I approach the mic.

Adrenaline's pumping. I feel fire building inside.

Nod to Jay D and Sultan, inhale deep,

glance at the crowd, their energy signals that they're ready for my truth.

Release my inhale . . . I'm ready too.

So I begin to give my spin

about what happened to me.

Speaking on the day that nearly took my youth.

My life flashed before me as I landed on the ground.

The cop's gun aimed; his voice so loud.

His finger caressed the trigger as he shouted, "STAY DOWN!"

The grim reaper waiting patiently to gather my soul.

I'm watching it all unfold like a 3-D scroll

as if is happening to some other dude instead of me.

I'm in a Black Lives state of mind.

If America looks away,

I'm gonna die in my prime.

The cops are out to get my kind.

Justice sees, but justice is blind.

Officers won't get indicted.

All the homies get excited.

Riots start erupting,

local-owned businesses get to burning,

young bloods out there looting.

More violence, more shootings, till the city's destitute and . . .

They'll say there ain't no resolution.

But BLM it ain't no passing phase.

We're no fad, we're here to stay.

We're no thugs, we're no gang.

We're here for solution; we're here for the change.

We're here to make sure there's never another hashtag trending beside a name.

We're here to raise

our signs so high and our voices so loud the caged birds hear us sing

"SAY THEIR NAMES" and "BLACK LIVES MATTER."

We're here to do away with the body bags and blood splatter.

To do away with the funeral arrangements and crying families.

We fill the streets and raise our voices in peace

until the blue shirts show up and spray us like fleas.

We welcome their presence like a Covid sneeze.

The media tells our stories, but the critics refuse

to accept the fate of our realities and claim fake news,

afraid to admit what we've been saying about systemic racism is true.

And so, it happens again and again to the women

and men in Black skin

by the women and men in blue.

I'm in a Black Lives state of mind.

If America looks away,

I'm gonna die in my prime.

The cops are out to get my kind.

Justice sees, but justice is blind.

We're not out here to settle a score.

We want equality across the board.

Pass the Mic

Jontrae runs up on stage.
I don't ask him what he's doing here
or about Tony's drop-the-mic contest.
He blurts, "I'm here,"
and I fill in the rest.
He knows this is where he should be.
We have an obligation to our craft
to use our voices
to rescue those on the warpath,
blinded by revenge,
who will turn this noble cause into a bloodbath.
I pass Jontrae the mic.
Jontrae begins to speak his truth.

To all my young bloods out there,
I understand your rage and despair.
With no justice, we're all at risk,
just waiting for our turn on the blacklist,
like a tourist in a war zone, I'm on edge,
knowing it only takes a small misstep
to become another name on the list
of lives taken unjustly, dismissed.
The justice system needs an overhaul,
it's time to answer the call,
to speak up, make our voices heard.
Justice is not just a word,
it's a right, a demand, a need,
so we stand together, united indeed,

BLM is here to stay.
We won't stop until justice has its day.

I'm in a Black Lives state of mind.
If America looks away,
I'm gonna die in my prime.
The cops are out to get my kind.
Justice sees, but justice is blind.

Jontrae looks over at me as if to say,
"I get it now."
The crowd is hyped.
I motion to the organizer to hand me a mic.
I join Jontrae as we chant with the demonstrators.

I'm in a Black Lives state of mind.
If America looks away,
I'm gonna die in my prime.
The cops are out to get my kind.
Justice sees, but justice is blind.

SIX MONTHS
LATER

Graduation

I'm still on the grind,
and I doubt that will ever change,
but I've changed.
Rap music is still important to me,
but not nearly as important as
seeing the way the police are communicating
with the people in our community.
I'd like to think I had something to do with that.
Today is graduation, and I've graduated from a lot of things.
I thought my senior year would be about senior privileges,
prom, the homecoming dance,
and pulling off an unforgettable senior prank,
but my senior year was better than I ever imagined.
It's not always about what you get.
Sometimes it's about what you leave behind.
Our poetry class was the first of its kind.
We had left behind a legacy of understanding
that our differences
are not nearly as important as
what we have in common.
We had broken through communication barriers,
paving the way for other classes to follow.
We had something better than a time capsule.
Breaking down barriers,
that was our legacy.
That was what we left behind.

ACKNOWLEDGMENTS

Thank you to my agent Katie Forbis, Stephanie Hansen, and the Metamorphosis Literary Agency; editors Michelle Halket, Beau Adler, Molly Ringle, and the Central Avenue Publishing staff for granting me this opportunity. Thank you to an amazing lyricist, Whitney Mitchell, for your contribution. I would also like to thank my father, John D. Roberts, my children, Wayne, Genesis, and Ivory for believing in and supporting my dream; my husband, Bryant; my sisters and sounding boards, Annette and Denice for your encouragement and support; my sisters Gwen, Gloria, and Elsie for all your help and support along this journey, my best friends Cheryl Berry, Angie Bennett, and Glenda Jones for the many ways you made this achievement possible; and also my best friend, Tammie Bunns, for celebrating this milestone with me; and Trinette Vereen for hosting my first indie author book signing.

This book is dedicated in loving memory of my mother, Geraldine Roberts, who was my biggest fan. Thanks for all the times you listened to me read WIPs. I wish you were here to walk into a bookstore and see my book on a shelf. You were a great writer, although many people never knew it. You inspired me to pursue my dream in ways words could never adequately express. This book is also dedicated in loving memory of Daisy Berry Burns. You were the first to tell me that you would someday walk into a bookstore and see my books and say, "Hey, I know that author." I am sorry you aren't here to see this day, but you believed it would happen, and it has.

Without faith, I would have given up a long time ago. Having said that, I thank my Lord and Savior, Jesus Christ for granting me strength and perseverance to see this project through to the end. May this book bring a greater understanding of the atrocities caused by racism. May we learn and grow from past mistakes and go on to make the world a better place for all people, regardless of race or ethnicity. To God be the glory!

A NOTE FROM LISA ROBERTS CARTER

Thank you for reading If You Knew My Name. I am grateful to everyone who came before me and left behind a legacy of faith, love, perseverance, and determination to be the change they wanted to see in the world. That is what I hope I left with you in this story.

It takes courage, conviction, and sacrifice to stand up and say this is not right, and I will be the change that is needed to tear down the walls racism has built. Book banning is not the solution. Ignoring or denying the problem won't make it go away. It'll only make it worse. Don't be afraid to have those hard conversations. After having them, take that next step toward change. Change is not always easy, but it is necessary to make the world a better place for all races. The journey of a thousand miles begins with a single step. I hope Mason Zy'Aire Tyndall has inspired you take that first step.

YOU MUST BE THE CHANGE YOU WISH TO SEE IN THE WORLD! — Mahatma Ghandi

Growing up in the rural South during desegregation, Lisa Roberts Carter is no stranger to racism — she recalls her mother and older sister having "the talk" with her on her very first day of school. Among the many reminders that racism was deeply embedded within her Southern culture, she experienced the residual effects of the Jim Crow South throughout her life. So, a frustrated Lisa decided to pen those thoughts, feelings, and experiences by writing historical and contemporary fiction that address racism and racial inequality. Lisa is a certified life and career coach and inspirational speaker with a Doctorate of Education. *If You Knew My Name* is her debut novel.